PENGUIN N

BLACK SUITS YOU

Novoneel Chakraborty is the author of fourteen bestselling thriller novels and one short story collection titled *Cheaters*. His novel *Forget Me Not, Stranger*, debuted as the No. 1 bestseller across India, while *All Yours, Stranger* ranked among the top-five thriller novels on Amazon India (the only one to feature amid other international bestsellers). His novel *Black Suits You* was in the top-five thrillers category on Amazon for fifteen weeks. While his Forever series was in the bestseller list for ten weeks straight after the release of *Forever Is a Lie*, which featured in the highest-selling-books list for 2017 on Flipkart. *Forever Is True* made it to Amazon's 'Memorable Books of 2017' and *Times of India*'s 'Most Stunning Books of 2017' lists.

Known for his novels featuring narrative twists, dark plots and strong female protagonists, Novoneel Chakraborty is also called the Sidney Sheldon of India by his readers. His immensely popular thriller series, the Stranger trilogy, has been translated into six Indian languages and has been adapted into a popular web series, titled *Hello Mini*, for MX Player, produced by Applause Entertainment and Rose Movies. His erotic thriller novel *Black Suits You* has been adapted into the blockbuster hit *Bekaaboo*, while his digital novella *Red Suits You* is also being adapted into a web series by ALTBalaji. His short story collection *Cheaters* is now available in Hindi as well. Apart from novels, Novoneel has written and developed several TV and web shows for premier channels and platforms. He lives and works in Mumbai.

BLACK
SUITS
YOU

NOVONEEL
CHAKRABORTY

Penguin
metro reads

An imprint of Penguin Random House

PENGUIN METRO READS

USA | Canada | UK | Ireland | Australia
New Zealand | India | South Africa | China

Penguin Metro Reads is part of the Penguin Random House group of companies
whose addresses can be found at global.penguinrandomhouse.com

Published by Penguin Random House India Pvt. Ltd
4th Floor, Capital Tower 1, MG Road,
Gurugram 122 002, Haryana, India

First published in Ebury Press by Penguin Random House India 2016
Published in Penguin Metro Reads 2021

Copyright © Novoneel Chakraborty 2016

All rights reserved

10 9 8 7

This is a work of fiction. Names, characters, places and incidents are either the
product of the author's imagination or are used fictitiously and any resemblance
to any actual person, living or dead, events or locales is entirely coincidental.

ISBN 9788184007909

Typeset in Requiem Text by Manipal Digital Systems, Manipal
Printed at Replika Press Pvt. Ltd, India

This book is sold subject to the condition that it shall not, by way of trade
or otherwise, be lent, resold, hired out, or otherwise circulated without the
publisher's prior consent in any form of binding or cover other than that in
which it is published and without a similar condition including this condition
being imposed on the subsequent purchaser.

www.penguinbooksindia.com

For Ishan
You bring back memories I don't remember

Prologue

'Did I ever tell you,' she asked softly on the phone, pressing the speaker close to her mouth so that her breathing was audible, 'The first thing that came to my mind when I saw you at the Delhi book event?'

'You didn't,' he replied, moistening his dry lips. He could imagine the way the words would manoeuvre her tongue before escaping her mouth.

'Imagine you and me lying naked beside each other—not even our shyness covers us—on a deserted rail track with our backs against the cold iron of the track. It's 3 a.m. We can't see anything beyond a few metres. It's just us with a dark night sky above. There's an eerie silence around and animal hunger within. Half a hunger in me, half a hunger in you.

'I slowly sit up, my hair hanging loose, looking at you all the while with thirsty eyes. I take your hands and pin them above you as I make myself comfortable on top of you—the cowgirl pose—and caress your hard-on. Its firmness accentuates my lust. Our eyes lock, looking deeply into each other as I raise myself just a bit to rub the tip of your penis around my wet vaginal lips and then slip it inside. The look on your face arouses me even more. It's an expression of our lust coalescing. The way you grab my ass with a sense of urgency makes me feel wanted. No guy can ever imagine what it is for a woman to feel desirable. It makes her feel like you are creating your own private world within her. As I gently bounce on you, my lips curl in and then out and my eyes roll back as if I'm losing myself, as if my flesh is vanishing, spool by spool. Remember I told you this world makes me feel like a house of concrete, but your touch—only *your* touch—makes me feel like a house of cards. It scares me, but then what's an arousal if not wrapped with unfelt emotions.

'I bend down. My loose hair falls just behind your head, forming a curtain around our faces. Sex is that unreal world where we discover the real us, isn't it? I take your tongue in my mouth and suck it hard. I rub my face on your chest, tracing its well-defined contours as my pelvic movement gains ferocity. I can feel our muscles tensing but there's something that calls for our attention. It's not our orgasms. Not yet. We both hear the sound of an approaching train. The iron track is vibrating slightly. The fear of getting run over only escalates the intensity of our carnal pleasure. As we rock harder, our mutual carnal chant is calling upon the impending climax. The train's light blinds us suddenly. Its shrill sound now seems deafening. It won't stop, we know, but it can't stop us either. Not for one second do we pause because this is all we want at the moment—communion. Right from the time we are born to the time we die, we need someone with us, within us, beside us. We can now read the fear of death in each other's eyes. But is it more than the unrealized love we seek through lust for each other? The train is getting dangerously close now. We cry out each other's names, only to be muted by the train. You hold my face, I hold yours. And together we close our eyes. Everything happens in slow motion—the train's speed, our rhythm, the closing of our eyes and the breeze that hits us. The train hollers past as we attain our spasmodic climax. We open our eyes to realize we are still alive. The train was on the track beside us.'

There was silence.

'That's how,' she continued, 'I wanted to take you.' She finally paused. The person on the other side was breathing heavily, as if he was still caught in the scene she had described.

'You there?' she asked.

'I want to meet you. Right. Now,' he said, swallowing a lump. He had never come across someone as wildly erotic as her.

'Are you sure?' she asked.

'Yes.'

'Remember, not every orgasm is about pleasure.'

'I don't give a fuck.'

Prologue

'All right then, come claim me. The way a warrior claims a kingdom.'

The line went dead. He thought he was getting into a casual affair. He was wrong. *Very, very wrong.*

Part 1: Seduce

1

India Habitat Centre, New Delhi
6 February 2016
Saturday, 6.30 p.m.

The stage was set. The PR and marketing team from the publishing house was present at the venue an hour before to supervise the arrangements. A few media personnel were also present, with their cameramen setting up equipment at the appropriate angles. There was an elevated wooden stage, with a huge the projector in the middle. Two chairs were placed in front of the projector, along with a table in between. One chair was for the moderator and one was for the 'star of the evening'. The table had a neatly made bouquet of red roses, two mineral water bottles, two copies of the box set of the trilogy and two mikes. The projector displayed a huge image of the book cover with the heading *Meet KIYAN ROY, the bestselling author of the sensational erotic trilogy* Handcuffs.

The initial print run of the first book had been twenty thousand. For a debut author attempting erotica—which has always been a prejudiced genre in India—it had been a decent print run. By the time the third book in the trilogy came out, the series had sold over sixty thousand copies. Kiyan wasn't the highest selling author in India yet, but the way his debut series had caught on with readers and non-readers alike was something that made him an author to watch out for. One of the reasons for the constant intrigue about the author himself was the fact that Kiyan was a social recluse. In this age of marketing and hype where people seldom tell stories but mostly sell them, Kiyan was an exception. Since the trilogy had come out, no reader had seen the writer behind the books. There was no photograph of him on the book or on the Internet. His social media was handled by the publisher's marketing team, and hence his and the trilogy's Facebook pages, Twitter handles and Instagram accounts were all about the books and nothing about him as a person. This made him all the more desirable to his female fan following. The men who read the trilogy learnt new ways to barter their horniness for maximum pleasure with their partners while the women found exciting fantasies to escape to when reality in the bedroom with their husbands or boyfriends bored them. And now, at the India Habitat Centre, the readers were going to see for the first time the author who had given

Indian readers a new subtext to the ever-so-hushed language of sex.

The publishing house wasn't initially sure how well the trilogy would sell. As someone once said, a book is a creative proposition till the author finishes it. After that, it is business. The publishing house had wanted to experiment with erotica to determine if it had a future as a genre in the contemporary Indian market, especially if it was written by an Indian. A couple of books that they had previously presented to readers as erotica had failed miserably. What Kiyan had done differently with his trilogy was to charge his writing with emotion, rather than use it as an excuse to garb vulgarity. This was the publishing house's final shot at the genre written by an Indian. As is the case with most writing, even mediocre erotica by a foreign writer is mostly welcome but gems by native writers need to undergo the test of acceptance. In Kiyan Roy, the publishers had finally found India's answer to E.L James and Sylvia Day. When they realized there was a buzz around the author and his work, they managed to convince Kiyan to go on a sponsored multi-city book tour to celebrate the trilogy's success and meet his readers, further enhancing the sales.

As people started pouring in, one person on the marketing team was counting the number of people in the room. As he finished, he had a big smile on his face. 269, with the majority being women. He quickly clicked a picture with his phone and sent it to the digital team, which uploaded it on their official Twitter, Facebook and Instagram accounts with the caption 'Delhi is ready for the man behind *Handcuffs*!'

The moderator was trying her best to keep the audience interested with some quiz about the trilogy as it was a little beyond the scheduled time and the event hadn't started yet. At around 6:43 p.m., Kiyan Roy appeared on stage to a loud cheer and applause. The girls could not take their eyes off him. It was as if something edible had just been dished up on stage.

'Ladies and gentleman, the man behind the books is finally here. Please welcome Kiyan Roy!' the moderator said, beaming from ear to ear.

There was a sudden blanket of silence.

'Hey everyone!' Kiyan spoke holding the mike close to his mouth as he settled in his chair amid a collective sigh from the audience. He was wearing a black Lucknowi chikan kurta with sleeves rolled up till his elbows, blue jeans and designer mojari sandals. His hair was parted to the left, and he was sporting thin black carbon-framed spectacles as well as a two-day-old stubble. Against his fair skin, the stubble gave him a rugged look.

'So, how does it feel to finally connect with your readers?' The moderator asked. She too had been waiting for this moment with bated breath. She couldn't help wondering how a person who had written such kinky stuff in *Handcuffs* would be in bed.

While some in the audience raised their phones to click pictures and a few chose to record the session, most of the women in the audience were mesmerised by Kiyan as he started responding to the moderator's question.

He is so handsome, thought one.

The way he constantly moistens his soft red lips while talking . . . uff, thought another.

OMG, his eyes . . . so naughty, so playful, so lively!

'Did you do any research before starting the trilogy?' asked the moderator.

'Since the genre was erotica, I secretly broke into couples' homes. You see, watching them make love was part of my research,' he said with a sarcastic smile.

The moderator didn't understand it was a joke but the audience did. They laughed out loud. The moderator followed.

Fuck, the guy has a sense of humour too, thought one of the girls. Her boyfriend sitting beside her glanced at her face and knew immediately he had competition.

'What would be the one thing you would tell young, aspiring authors?' the moderator asked.

'I would say they should live the stories they want to write.'

'Did you live *Handcuffs?*'

'Not entirely, of course, but a part of it, yes. In fact, the seed of the idea of the trilogy came from a friend, Tina Awasthi.'

'How wonderful!' exclaimed the moderator and continued, 'I know most girls here wish they could be a muse for someone like you.'

'You never know when that can happen.'

'One question which I guess is on every girl's mind here is . . .'

There was silence.

'Are you single, Kiyan?'

Kiyan blushed slightly as he said, 'I am.'

Someone in the crowd whistled, which triggered laughter from everyone.

The Q&A session with the moderator went on for half an hour, after which Kiyan was available to sign copies of his books as well as click selfies. The recluse in Kiyan felt awkward every time a girl stood close to him and asked her husband or boyfriend to click a picture. But he suffered all the awkwardness and embarrassing remarks like 'I wish my boyfriend had a sexual quotient as high as yours' with a bright smile. The entire event wrapped up by 8 p.m. The managing director along with the team of editors and marketing team took Kiyan for a sumptuous dinner at Aqua at The Park. From the latest publishing world gossip and how boring the newest superhero franchise movie was to the bombing in Syria, everything was discussed and opinions were exchanged over drinks, sheesha, risottos and chocolate brownies.

'So when are you pitching us your next erotic tale?' Natasha, Kiyan's editor, asked as they walked to their cars in the parking lot. The others had already bid goodbye.

'I'm on the lookout for a story. Let's see when it meets me.'

'Make it fast, Kiyan. Everyone in our team is with you. We don't want to lose out on the momentum the trilogy has created. One book a year is a must. And it's February already. You have to submit by May so that we can schedule the book for November this year.'

'I get it. You shall have a synopsis very soon.'

'That's great,' Natasha said, unlocking her car. 'Give me something bigger and sexier than *Handcuffs*, if you know what I mean.'

'I do,' Kiyan said with a smirk. They hugged. Natasha drove out of the parking while Kiyan was driven to his hotel by his appointed chauffeur for the day.

In the hotel, Kiyan checked out all the gifts given to him by the readers—flowers, cards, shot glasses etc. He took a hot shower next, freshened up, made some calls and switched on the television, ensconced in the cosy bed. Just then, the hotel landline rang. Kiyan took the call.

'Sorry to disturb you, sir. I'm calling from the reception.'

'What is it about?'

'Someone has just left a pen drive with us and asked to deliver it to you. If you are free, may I send someone upstairs right now?'

'A pen drive?'

'That's right, sir.'

'Who left it?'

'The person didn't mention any name except for the fact that you would understand who it is.'

'Oh. Send it upstairs.'

'Right sir.'

Kiyan was puzzled what the pen drive could be about and who could have sent it. Was it *her*? There was a knock on the door. Kiyan promptly opened it. A hotel staffer handed him a tiny pen drive.

'Thanks,' Kiyan said and closed the door. He looked at it inquisitively for a moment and then reached into his bag to take out his laptop. Inserting the pen drive into one of the USB ports, he sat down on the chair in the room, stretching his legs out on the bed. After the pen drive was read and scanned for viruses, he noticed a single folder on the drive. It was titled 'Love is in the Details'. A curious smile appeared on Kiyan's face as it was the working title of his trilogy before it was released as *Handcuffs*. *It had to be her*, he thought and clicked open the folder. There were, Kiyan counted, 13 pictures of his from the book event. As he clicked on each one, he noticed they focussed on his features. One was a close-up of his tongue coming out of his mouth to moisten his lips, one had captured his smirk, another his fingers, yet others of the biceps covered by his black kurta, his eyebrows and the like. The pictures were so precise and well-framed that they looked like paintings. With a jolt, he noticed that every picture had a single alphabet scrawled on it—u, i, o, c . . . Whoever had sent it knew his penchant for word puzzles. He grabbed the pencil kept beside the room's phone and quickly jotted down those alphabets on the notepad lying close by. It took him four minutes to crack the words those alphabets could have been possibly arranged into. It read: *Black Suits You.*

Kiyan immediately called up the reception.

'Hi, I'm calling from room 611. Could you please tell me if it was a girl or a boy who gave you the pen drive?'

'It was a girl, sir,' the receptionist said.

* * *

A Girl's Diary

6 February 2016
Saturday, 11.13 p.m.

A human being can fall for another. Age, sex and background have nothing to do with it. People try to define a protocol for every phenomenon. We can't see anything as limitless or infinite. To understand the infinite, we limit it and bring it under the finite scope of our understanding because it's we who have limitations. Natural things like love don't. They can't.

I often wonder, at which point does a love story really begin? Does it begin when the individuals involved see each other for the first time? Or, when they start thinking about each other in the days that follow. Or, when they meet up for the first time after they have thought about the other? And revel, in the nights that follow, in the suddenly realized joy of one's own heart that was hitherto unleashed. Or, when they start talking at length and discover how similar or different they are, depending on whatever excites them more. Or, when they begin to know each other with every passing meeting and surrender, quite involuntarily, to the mystery that the other person seems to be. Or, do they simply fall in love when they are meant to fall in love? Like when they come together and there's no alternative but for a love story to begin.

I guess ours began because it was destined to. It happened on 2 November 2005 at around seven in the evening by the only ATM outlet of a nationalized bank a few metres from the sprawling campus of the private Jamuna Bai

College of Engineering and Management in Wakhnaghat, Solan, in Himachal Pradesh where I was completing my engineering. I was trying to withdraw cash from the standalone ATM that evening before the suddenly announced Diwali holidays, when I found my debit card being sucked in by the machine. I panicked and went out, trying to spot the security guard, but there was nobody around. There was no bank either nearby where I could lodge a complaint or ask someone to open up the ATM machine to retrieve the card. I was panicking because I was there to take out cash for the middleman, Ramesh, who used to do all the Tatkaal tickets for the students' homebound trips during the holidays. He was waiting outside my college. He would collect the cash from students, write down their names and provide them their respective confirmed tickets the following evening. Without the cash, I wouldn't have been able to go home on that Diwali.

With the security guard gone, who otherwise paced up and down in front of the ATM either playing Altaf Raja songs aloud on his mobile phone, sleeping, staring at the college girls or at times sharing a cigarette or two with the college guys,

I came back inside the ATM. Anxious, I started tapping all the buttons on the machine, hoping that the card would come out on its own. But it didn't. I looked at the ATM door because I had heard someone knock. I could see a pair of legs in rugged jeans waiting outside the ATM. The person's face wasn't visible from inside because of a couple of printouts pasted on the glass door citing certain bank rules. The knock sounded again and this time with ascended urgency. Before I could react, the person pushed open the door and peeped in.

'Excuse me, but are you looting the machine or something, because you are taking way too much time?' he asked.

If he thought he had cracked some wise-ass joke, then he was wrong. I found it rude.

'I'm sorry, but the machine sucked in my card,' I told him.

'Oh!' He now stepped inside the ATM without really being invited and checked the machine himself by pressing a few buttons. When nothing happened, he stood there contemplating, with one hand folded and the other perched on his chin.

'Either your card has expired or there's some problem with the machine,' he said.

'It's my father's card,' I exclaimed. 'I don't know if it has expired or not.'

'Call the bank's customer care.'

'I don't have the customer care number.'

'We can get it off the Internet. No big deal. But first, you should let your father know about it.'

'I will, but . . .'

'But?'

I moved the hair out of my face with my hand and continued, 'But right now, I need cash. I only had this card with me.'

'By any chance, do you need cash for Ramesh?'

I looked at him incredulously and asked, 'You too?'

He inserted his card with an ironical smile and withdrew the cash from the machine.

'Yes. My friends are lazy bums and wanted me to collect the cash for them too. Anyway, how much do you need?'

'Six hundred,' I murmured with embarrassment.

'Here.'

'Sorry but I can't take that.'

'It's okay. I'm charging each of my friends fifty bucks extra as interest since I'm paying for their tickets. So it's their money actually.'

I hesitated momentarily, then smiled tightly, realizing that he was joking about the interest and he wanted to help me out after all.

'Thanks. I'll return it soon,' I said and took the cash.

'Please do, else I'll charge high interest—steaming momos every weekend.'

I smiled just like he did.

'I think I can afford that much interest,' I said, pushing the ATM door open.

'Just my luck then,' he said and stretched out his hand, 'Kiyan Roy, Mechanical, third year.'

I told him my name. And we shook hands. Did you notice how from 'I' and 'him' suddenly it arrived at 'we'? Was that the precise beginning of our love story? I think it was.

2

Starmark Book Store, South City Mall, Kolkata
13 February 2016
Saturday, 7.00 p.m.

'There is a game of sorts for everyone present today,' the emcee said aloud on the mike. Nobody looked at her. All eyes, from the time Kiyan had come in front and taken a seat after unwrapping the bestselling edition of the trilogy box set, were trained on him. And they looked at him with broadly three emotions—awe, respect and lust. Though Kiyan was Bong, his roots were in UP, not Bengal. And this was the first time he was visiting Kolkata. He was in casual attire this time, a black round-collared tee accompanied by torn blue jeans with Converse shoes. His red-bordered Calvin Klein underwear was peeping out slightly from the low-waist jeans. As he turned to take his seat, many girls checked out his firm ass over the jeans and moistened their lips.

Everyone in the audience was handed a paper chit and asked to write a question of their choice that they had always wanted to ask the author.

'And there's no need to write one's name on it either. The lucky ones will have their questions answered,' the emcee announced.

A total of 170 chits were put inside a big glass bowl and presented to Kiyan. He smiled as he picked up one of the chits. He unfolded it. His eyebrows were raised as he read the question out aloud on his mike.

'What's your size?'

The crowd burst into laughter.

'And let me add,' said the emcee beaming, 'that you can't take much time before answering.'

'It's 42.'

Everyone's jaw fell open.

'Since nothing was specified, I presume whoever asked this wanted to know my shirt size, right?'

Half the crowd laughed while the other half expressed disappointment

'That's true actually. We hope the other questions are specific,' the emcee said and requested Kiyan to pick up another chit.

He read out the next one, 'Are you committed?'

'Every author has an alter ego. If the author is committed, the alter ego is single. If the author is single the alter ego is committed,' Kiyan said and looked at everyone.

'Confused?' he asked.

The crowd cried out a collective 'Yes!'

'Good. Let's keep it that way,' he said. Anyone who had an issue with the evasive reply forgave him when they saw his charming smile.

Kiyan was quick to pick up the next chit.

'Why does a relationship fail?' he read aloud.

'Not that I'm some kind of relationship expert, but I believe sometimes the speed of a relationship in our mind is more than the speed of a relationship for real.'

'That's interesting. Could you please clarify a bit more for us Kiyan?' the emcee insisted.

'Sure. What I mean is what we commit to easily is often an illusion. The thing we know as love-at-first-sight is an illusion. To love is to know, to understand. You can't fall in love and then understand someone because there is a very high possibility your understanding is biased. You can know someone and fall in love during the process. So, from the time we say it's love-at-first-sight, we are simply committing ourselves to an illusion that in no time seems like reality. And when illusion becomes reality for anyone, he or she is bound to head towards a failed relationship sooner or later.'

'So, in a nutshell, what you are saying is one should understand what is real and then commit to it.'

'Precisely. All I'm saying is if you want a healthy relationship then embrace what is and not what should be.'

Novoneel Chakraborty

There was mild applause. As Kiyan took time to pick the next chit from the glass bowl, he noticed a girl standing right behind the last row of seats among a few others, with a DSLR camera pointed at him. Their eyes met after she finished clicking. She smiled at him. The intent with which she did so made him ask himself, *could she be the girl who sent the pen drive with the close-ups? From a New Delhi book launch to Kolkata?* Kiyan wondered. *Maybe she studied in New Delhi and lived in Kolkata. Or maybe vice versa. Or maybe . . . how does it matter?* But the incident had registered with him. An author's mind is always curious about anything untoward. And the close-ups along with the word puzzle were weird enough to pique his interest. He smiled back faintly and picked up another chit.

'What is a story according to you?' he read aloud.

Kiyan took a deep breath before he spoke, 'Let me first tell you all that there is nothing called a good story or a bad story. There is a story you believe in and a story you don't believe in. That's the best thing about art actually. Better than science. Art is malleable, not science. Art is subjective, unlike science. Art is not conclusive. Science always needs to be so. Answering the question, I would say . . .' For a moment, he went blank when he saw the same girl gaping at him in a way as if she was lost in him. Not that he hadn't seen such faces during the New Delhi crowd, but what he knew about this girl was she had a penchant for details. What was she noticing right now? Kiyan wondered and heard the emcee clear her throat softly.

'I would say a story is a dangerous entity, as often it acts as a mirror to what we have been avoiding for a long time. That's also why reading is such a personal experience.'

'How wonderfully true that is!' the emcee said. The expressions on everyone's faces told Kiyan that they agreed. He picked another chit and read aloud, 'I came to know that a girl named Tina gave you the idea for the trilogy. Is it true? And where is she now?'

'Well, that's true. Tina Awasthi is a friend. However, she planted the seed pretty unknowingly. I'm not in touch with her at present, but I hope wherever she is, she reads the trilogy.'

A few acknowledging smiles later, it was time for the next chit.

'Any tips for budding authors?' Kiyan read aloud.

'Live your story before you write it. For then you would be closer to the character's emotions. Be the character for some time, even if it is in your head. Then, it will translate into your narrative. That's all I would say.'

Someone raised a hand in the crowd. That someone was the same person who had been aiming the DSLR at him time and again. The emcee gestured for her to ask the question. A bookstore employee handed over the mike to her.

'Does that mean you've experienced what's written in *Handcuffs*?'

'In the trilogy, my protagonist screws with his own girlfriend's trust, someone's fiancé and his female boss. Did I experience it all? Of course not!' he said with a naughty smile. People echoed his smile.

'I'm sorry, I didn't get what exactly you meant by live your story?' the girl asked.

'It means, whatever happens in your story should happen in your head and affect you with the same emotional vibrancy as it would affect your characters. Then, you don't remain an author, an outside force, a voyeur to your characters but become their confidante... someone who is within them. That's the most difficult challenge for any author—to get under the skin of their characters. Once that's done, everything else flows from there.'

'Thanks.' She smiled.

'Cheers.' He smiled back. Their eyes remained locked for a tad longer than they should have.

A few more questions were answered by Kiyan, after which the emcee announced that Kiyan would sign books for the crowd. An immediate queue was formed. Kiyan was signing copies a little faster than he had in New Delhi, giving the readers a constant smile and appeasing their selfie requests. Never did he lose track of the girl with the DSLR who was somewhere in the middle of the line. In no time, she came face to face with Kiyan. He took the three books from her and asked, 'Your name please?'

'Mitakshi.'

'Nice name,' Kiyan said as he signed the first book for her. *To Mitakshi, with love*, he wrote.

'Thank you so much. Even your protagonist's name starts with M in the trilogy.'

'Indeed.' Kiyan paused and then opened the second book of the trilogy to sign on it. He was about to write the same thing when Mitakshi stopped him. 'Could you please write something different in each book?' She looked at him intently, and he couldn't say no.

'Sure.'

You have an amazing smile. Keep smiling, he wrote and signed.

'Oh my God!' Mitakshi said and kept staring as Kiyan signed the third book for her. This time a little slowly.

'You will be having dinner tonight, right?' Mitakshi said. Kiyan, from the corner of his eye could see her hands, clasping her clutch and DSLR, were shaking a bit.

'Of course I will. Like a normal human being.'

'Please tell me you are dining alone.' Mitakshi made a puppy face. Kiyan understood what she had in mind. Unlike New Delhi, there wasn't anyone from the publishing house with whom he was supposed to dine. All he had to do after the event was head back to the hotel, eat alone and sleep. He gave Mitakshi a glance. She was an attractive girl.

'Actually, I'm not dining alone,' Kiyan said. Mitakshi's face immediately fell.

'Someone whose name starts with M is going to join me,' Kiyan said with amusement in his eyes.

'May I please die?' Mitakshi said and quickly added, 'I'll wait for you.' She took her books and stepped aside. As Kiyan signed the books for others, she kept staring at him the way one stares at a moonlit sky, awed by it.

In the next hour, the two were sitting opposite each other in Hakuna Matata, in Park Street. Mitakshi was the one who talked the most. And the more she talked, the more Kiyan felt she was childlike. She had a very different mental wavelength, perception and outlook. And he didn't like girls. He liked women. He loved ladies. He adored matured, independent, opinionated and controlling women. Thus most of what Mitakshi spoke was forgotten immediately. And all he did through the dinner was nod a little, smile a bit and project that he was enjoying her company. Though Mitakshi insisted, Kiyan didn't share his phone number with her. He had had enough of her already, he thought. Kiyan wrapped the dinner up within an hour, bade her goodbye and returned to the hotel.

When Kiyan had been sent the close-ups in a pen drive, he had assumed there would be a sexy mind behind it, but he had found it to be bland. He was disappointed that he had judged wrong. As he headed up to his room and was about to close his door behind him, he heard someone say, 'Excuse me, sir.'

It was the laundry person. Kiyan opened the door as the guy went inside and kept all the clothes that Kiyan had asked be washed and ironed on the table.

'It's okay. I need to pack them,' Kiyan said, seeing the laundry guy trying to keep the clothes in the cupboard. The guy smiled at him and left the room. Kiyan opened his American Tourister suitcase and lifted the pile of clothes up from the table and placed it inside the suitcase. He turned around and noticed a small bunch was still on the table. It was his underwear. He wore Calvin Klein briefs. He picked them up and was about to put them in the suitcase when he stopped, noticing a piece of paper hanging from one of his black briefs. As he took it in his hand, he realized it was a small card attached by a black thread.

You said one should know the difference between illusion and reality. You pursued an illusion. I thought you were smarter than this, Mister Bestselling Author. Chase the reality. Chase me.

A few seconds later, Kiyan's thoughtful look changed into a smirk. Whoever it was knew pretty well that he loved games of this kind. He was glad Mitakshi wasn't the girl who had clicked those pictures of him.

* * *

A Girl's Diary

13 February 2016
Saturday, 11.50 p.m.

The following night, after Kiyan helped me
with the ticket money, I was in the sixth
bogie of the Chandigarh-Lucknow Express,
which left Chandigarh at precisely 8.50 p.m.
My entire girl gang was possessed by the
thrill of going home. This was the longest
we had been away, ten months. Last time we
had been home was on Holi. And now it was
Diwali. Being with parents was a part of
the thrill. It was the fact that we would
get to sleep away half the day, eat mom-
made food and secretly drink vodka & 7Up
for half the night with friends without any
tension of going to the college the next
day that made us so eager for the homebound
journey. Add to that, we had decided to
meet at one of our friend's place and play
cards with proper money during Diwali. The
wager was that the winner had to throw a
booze party for all of us.

It was around one at night that I suddenly
awoke on my upper side berth. Someone had

entered the sleeper class from the toilet outside and struck my feet spilling out of the berth. It was good because I anyway wanted to get up to pee and smoke. I climbed down, wore my slippers and collected my cigarette packet and lighter from my bag on the way out. I was about to cross over from the compartment to the toilet when I noticed someone standing by one of the train doors. He had a cigarette in his hand and was taking a long puff. As he exhaled and casually turned around, he noticed me.

'Hey,' I said, hoping he would recognize me. To this day, I don't exactly know why I said that. Why did I initiate a conversation? Agreed he was the same guy who had helped me with the ATM card, but still.

'Hi.' The way his eyes, for a second, stayed on my cigarette told me he hadn't expected me to be a smoker.

'I don't smoke often.' I couldn't reason with myself why I lied to him. What would I want to gain from that lie?

'Good. Smoking is bad,' Kiyan said and threw his cigarette out. 'I too smoke rarely.' He came to stand opposite me by the other end of the door. It was funny how we two almost strangers were trying to justify our smoking habit to each other.

There was a strong wind blowing on our faces. I was finding it difficult to keep my hair away from my face. I saw him look at me the way you do when you adore something. It made me nervous and at the same time feel desired too.

'And that rare instance occurs due to peer pressure, you know.' He was still talking about his smoking habit.

'I believe you do what you want to do.' I was always a cut-to-the-chase kind of girl. He kept looking at me as if he didn't expect me to say it. To be honest, there was something genuine about this guy who had helped me in the ATM. But as the golden rule goes, you never know with a guy. I thought of testing Kiyan to see if he really was sincere or just another prudent Indian male who couldn't see a girl doing the so-called manly thing.

'Have you asked your friends who smoke not to do so as well?'

Kiyan gaped at me for a moment before saying, 'No.'

Another chauvinist! I was almost about to conclude when Kiyan's retort steered my mind to a complete different conclusion.

'I read somewhere that when a girl smokes, especially young girls, it affects their system to an extent that it may affect the foetus whenever she conceives. I don't know if it's correct or not but then why take a risk. It's a matter of two lives, yours and your baby's.'

'Thanks for the information. I was so planning to get pregnant this Diwali.'

His jaw dropped open. And I couldn't help my laughter.

'It was a . . . joke,' I clarified. Finally, he laughed with me.

'Sorry if I sounded patronizing,' he said.

'No issues. By the way, you were right. The debit card had expired. I'll get a replacement this time, and I'll give you your money after the Diwali holidays.'

'That's all right.' Kiyan moistened his lips. The train seemed to have picked up speed in the last few minutes.

'Are you going to Lucknow or getting down somewhere in between?' I asked.

'Lucknow. What about you?'

'Lucknow,' I said.

The silence that followed told me we needed to continue asking each other questions lest one of us said 'excuse me' and went away. This urge to stretch a conversation with a guy was also a first for me.

Thankfully for me, he asked, 'Which school did you go to in Lucknow?' I wasn't yet ready for him to know I was interested. In the beginning, it is always better not to be too obvious about your intentions.

'Cathedral School in Hazrat Ganj,' I replied.

'We were neighbours then. I was in St Francis,' Kiyan said coyly.

'Funny. We were so close but never met.'

'Obviously. We didn't know each other. There was no context.'

Now we have a context, I wondered, *and life never creates context in someone's life out of context.*

'Where do you stay?' he asked.

'Jopling Road. And you?'

'Aliganj.'

Yet another silence fell. A bit more prolonged than the last. And it seemed to communicate something more than our words did.

'I was thinking that there's a way of giving me the money sooner too,' he said.

I kind of guessed what was coming. All boys are actually predictable. And probably that's where their cuteness lies, unlike us girls whose charm is cocooned in our unpredictability. I kept quiet and allowed Kiyan to finish.

'We can meet up in Lucknow during the Diwali holidays,' he said, matching my expectations.

I caught a glimpse of myself on the small mirror atop the wash basin on the side. The twinkle in my eyes and the tinge of his faint smile told me our story had finally begun.

3

Kiyan's was a little wary at the book event in Crossword. Two words were constantly ricocheting in his head, *Chase me*. He had torn the note into three pieces before throwing it into the garbage dump. What on earth did it mean anyway? Why would he chase her? This was someone who had attended one of his book events, no, two book events, and then disappeared throughout the week. He knew nothing about her except that she, in all probability, was a reader of his books. Like so many others. What was so special about her? A second later, he answered it himself. The special thing was that she actually made him think about her, unlike the rest.

There was also slight anger burning in him. And its flame wasn't directed towards the girl but towards himself. How could he be so dumb? He had taken

Mitakshi out for dinner because he thought she was the one who had sent him the photographs even though he had neither asked Mitakshi about it nor had she claimed anything of the sort. How could he have been so presumptuous? For a twenty-seven-year-old, it was silly. Also, the actual person who was stalking him across book events would know how easy he was. He had violated the golden rule he had once learnt from one of his marketing team guys—easy is cheesy. And a celebrity can't be easy. Not with his/her fans. There should be a mystery, a myth attached to the celebrity. The fans desire the celeb only because of that fantastic, unbridgeable distance. By distance, the marketing person didn't mean physical distance, but rather the mystery behind the persona. With Kiyan goofing up with Mitakshi, he was sure the girl who had sent him the photos must have realized that Kiyan wasn't all that smart. But all said and done, he had to answer only one question now—does it really matter? Who the fuck is this girl anyway? Let her assume whatever she wants to assume. He never claimed that he had mistaken Mitakshi for her. And he didn't need to respond to her 'chase-me' game.

Kiyan went to the book launch with the conviction that he didn't give a damn about the girl. It was new-found fame for him, and he was sure these things would happen in the future too. He better get used to it without taking everything too seriously. However, he couldn't stop his eyes scanning the room, trying to look for the mysterious someone during the book event. He had read about and begun to believe in the superstition that what happens twice happens for the third time as well. The fact that he was giving an unknown person so much of his mental space was disturbing Kiyan. He was simply unable to erase the echo of those two words—'chase me'—from his mind, even though he had debated the futility of it.

When Kiyan had read the note last weekend at the hotel in Kolkata, it had seemed casual, but now in his mind, it called out to him like a challenge, like he wouldn't be a man if he didn't chase her after thinking about her so much

After the event got over, Kiyan had a quick chat with the sales guy from his publishing house and learnt that the trilogy had gone for a tenth impression. He wanted to go back to the hotel to sleep when he received a WhatsApp message from Natasha asking him if he'd zeroed in on an idea for his next book yet.

I have. Though a little vague as of now.

He was bluffing. He didn't want to sound like he had become creatively bankrupt after the debut trilogy. A quick way of generating a story and subsequently a one-line pitch for it is to ask yourself what is happening in your life at the moment. Kiyan thought about it and started muttering under his breath, 'Trilogy success . . . bestseller . . . book events . . . someone trying to approach him . . . a fan?'

What about a sexy story of a bestselling debut author and one of his readers?

Wonderful. Any hints? Natasha asked.

A bestselling author and a diehard fan-cum-stalker, Kiyan typed then wondered, *would the girl stalking him really give him a story?* The thought aroused him creatively. Authors being selfish people, they seek stories in their own emotional debris as well as in other people's. Natasha had once explained to him that to commercialize what is personal often brings authors a lot of fame. Whether it is good fame or bad fame doesn't matter because personal stories give readers a chance to connect emotionally.

I'll soon let you know, Kiyan WhatsApped back. Was he using his new-found storyline as an excuse to give himself a reason to keep thinking about the girl who wrote to him those two words: *chase me?* Kiyan avoided the question in his mind as if it had never occurred to him. Right after the event, he called his driver and asked him to come up to the bookstore exit. He collected all the gifts and bouquets and looked around one more time. There was nobody suspicious enough for him to look at twice.

'Yeah, the event went well.' Kiyan was on phone as he climbed out of his car. 'The bookstore was in Aundh, which is close to Pune city. The events are fun. Not what I thought they would be.' Kiyan crossed the road to enter the Rude Lounge building and waited for the elevator to arrive.

'No, I'm not in the hotel. I came to a nearby lounge. Natasha, my editor, said I need to give her a synopsis for my next soon.

'No, I don't have a story yet but just a vague idea. I want it to start at a nightclub actually. So, let's see. Yeah I'll call you later. Bye.'

Kiyan got off the phone and stepped into the elevator. He pressed the fifth floor button. Unlike others, he could never pretend to focus on his phone when in public because he had no social media apps on it. He used to be on them earlier, but with time, he had lost touch with his school and college friends. Social networking sites, as he had come to understood, were more of a pseudo connection. True, they helped people trace long-lost friends, but that was about it. After the tracing was done, if one really wanted to stay in touch, a phone number was enough. The rest was all about the gratification of the voyeur monster that lives latent within us all, constantly feeding off the events in others' lives. Moreover, he liked observing people in public rather than checking updates on his phone.

Kiyan moved out of the elevator, extended his hand to be stamped by a bouncer and entered the lounge space. Most of the lounge was a dance floor with couches at various corners and a good bar space at the left of the entrance. Kiyan had chosen this particular lounge because it had a rooftop. He felt claustrophobic otherwise. He went to the bar and ordered a Jack and Coke, and looked around for an empty spot.

Kiyan wasn't a party animal but sitting with a drink and looking at people dancing to music amused him. It was a sight that told him society wound people up into knots while they let themselves loosen up in a place like this. Music with alcohol was a winning combination for this to happen. But not for Kiyan. He never wanted to let go. He liked control. He liked to be in his senses, to be in charge. Sights like these always worked as triggers for stories. As he sipped his Jack and Coke, Kiyan heard a collective hoot from the clubbers as he saw a girl in a one-piece, figure-hugging blue dress get on top of the bar counter and dance to the ongoing Punjabi rap. Could she be his next character? He wondered. Her dance had a certain wildness to it that aroused Kiyan's creativity. Like she didn't give a fuck about what people thought about her. So very unlike him. She had an arresting appeal about her even though Kiyan couldn't see her face clearly. He kept eyeing the girl and observing her moves, her messy hairdo, the dollops of sweat shining on her bare shoulder and thighs, the curves underlined by her dress and the way the disc lights were falling on her. They lit her up like a true fantasy, a muse. She took a bow as the rap ended, while people hooted and whistled for her. Kiyan wanted to approach her, to know her just that much that it would help add colour to the character he had roughly sketched in his mind in the last one minute. But before he could spot her, she mingled into the crowd.

Kiyan went to the bar for a refill, eyes constantly trying to spot the girl. As the bartender filled his glass, Kiyan felt a tap on his shoulder. He turned around, but no one was standing there. He assumed someone must have brushed against him. He took his glass and went back to the same corner, only to see the seat had been taken by a couple who were busy smooching. Kiyan momentarily considered asking for his seat back, but their passion made it clear it was better to leave them alone. He looked around and spotted an empty couch in a corner where the multiple disco lights were shining incessantly. He went over and was about to sit when a girl came and sat down with a thud. Kiyan was immediately alert.

'Sorry,' she said and shifted just a bit to make space for Kiyan.

'Not a problem.' He noticed her dress and realized it was the same girl who had danced on the bar minutes ago. He tried but couldn't see her face since she was bending down, fiddling with her stiletto. Kiyan sat down beside her, still observing her from the corner of his eye.

'You came here alone?' the girl asked, without looking at Kiyan.

'Yes.' A pause later, he added, 'And you?'

'Alone.' She was still fidgeting with her stiletto.

'Any problem?' Kiyan asked.

'The stupid heel broke when I was dancing.'

'I saw that.'

'You saw the heel break?' This time, the girl turned to glance at Kiyan. The way her hair fell on her face increased the initial attraction he had felt for her to a different level. With blue, red and golden disco lights falling on the other rest of her face, he couldn't make out her natural look.

'I saw you dance on that bar top.' He had to lean forward a bit to be audible.

The girl gave him an acknowledging nod and took her stiletto off. He couldn't decide whether her shapely feet or the dark nail paint on the toenails were more beautiful. She stretched her feet slightly as if they were hurting her and then started massaging her calf.

There are people with whom you love to talk and there are people with whom you love the silence. The latter was true with this girl. They weren't talking, but every action of hers was like new information for Kiyan. It felt like he was getting to know her from the way she took off her stiletto, the way she moved, the way she touched her calf and pressed it while tucking part of her hair behind her ears; every action of hers had a sexy narrative to it. Kiyan didn't realize when he finished his second Jack and Coke. He tried to get up to fetch another glass but fell back on the couch. He closed his eyes shut tight once and then opened them to realize his head was reeling slightly while the images of people dancing, the lights and the noise were all progressively turning fuzzy. He felt a hand on his shoulder. It was the girl. She was telling him something, but he couldn't hear her clearly. Everything seemed like a lucid dream where he knew he was present but nothing was registering in his mind. The girl put one of his arms around her shoulders and helped him move out of the lounge. A bouncer came to help but she told him he was her boyfriend and she was capable of taking care of him herself. Kiyan, by then, had slipped into semi-consciousness.

Once out of the lounge, the girl took Kiyan to a car. She unlocked it and made him comfortable on the front seat. She quickly climbed into the driver's seat and drove the car to a mostly secluded place. They sat still, she waiting impatiently for a couple to pass by. The moment the couple's reflection disappeared from the rear-view mirror, she turned to Kiyan. Looking at him hungrily, she licked her lips twice. She reached across him and pressed a button by the window, making Kiyan's seat recline. He was constantly blabbering something, but none of it made sense. She looked straight into his semi-open, rolled-up eyes and made herself comfortable on top of him, putting her knees on his sides. She drew close to his face and touched his forehead with her nose. She dragged the tip of her nose from his forehead to his chin and then to his chest, inhaling his fragrance as if she was inhaling life. She didn't breathe out immediately.

She held her breath like she was allowing his fragrance to permeate through her. After some seconds, she leaned forward once again and exhaled softly on his face. One by one, she unbuttoned his shirt till his torso was bare. Placing her face on his bare chest, she started rubbing her face across it, breathing out hard and feeling her passion escalate. On an impulse, she bit him right on his chest and dug her teeth deep into his flesh until she was sure it would leave a mark. As she sat up staring at the bite mark, she sucked in her cheeks and wondered, *The taste of you is even better than your thoughts, mister bestselling author*. She giggled naughtily and bent down to suck his lips.

* * *

A Girl's Diary

20 February 2016, 11.58 p.m.

It was the day after Diwali that Kiyan called me on my mobile phone. I was waiting for it.

'Hey, how is Diwali going?' he asked. It felt nice to hear his voice. For the first time, I realized someone else's actions can tell you a lot about yourself. Like the call from Kiyan told me, conclusively, that a part of me had been waiting for it; a part that had been asking a lot of questions since we met at the ATM and then in the night train. But I chose not to answer them. Not yet.

'Good. And yours?' I asked.

'Great. Diwali is actually that time of the year when almost all my cousins are here. So it's really fun.'

I sensed relief in his voice, as if he had wanted to make the call for a long time but wasn't sure how I would react.

'Same here. More than the festival, it's the get-together that is more enjoyable.'

'And the sweets from Ramasrey!' he added, sounding like a kid.

'Bongs and their love for sweets,' I said. He laughed. I could imagine him do so. In fact, I'd observed him acutely in the train. It had helped me imagine him a lot since that night.

'More than sweets, I indulge in the chaat they serve at King Chaat in Hazrat Ganj,' I said.

'Oh yes, I love chaat too,' he replied. It sounded like he was weighing his words before saying them.

'Actually . . .' Kiyan said, 'I don't like chaat much.'

It was my turn to laugh out aloud. I wanted to pull his cheeks for the cute confession.

'Then why didn't you say so before?' I was finding it hard to control my laughter.

'Well . . . you know . . . ummm.'

'Yeah, okay, I got that,' I said to calm his awkwardness. Of course he had said it to look like we were similar. Something guys often do to make the girl like them. But the immediate confession made him stand out from the ones I had seen or heard about.

'By the way, aren't you supposed to be in Kolkata or something? Or are you a Lucknow native?' I questioned, deliberately steered the conversation.

'The last three generations of my family have been settled in Lucknow. Never been to Kolkata actually.'

'Okay.'

There was a sudden silence. I didn't know what else to say and probably he too was wondering the same.

'When are we meeting, Kiyan?' I blurted out, without thinking it could have been misinterpreted by him.

'Oh,' he was clearly not ready for it. 'You tell me,' he continued. 'I'm free, except for at night.'

'I won't be able to meet you at night anyway. Parents won't allow. How about Royal Cafe at around five in the evening today?'

'Great!'

We were done with the phone conversation. Honestly, I was yet to meet a boy outside of school or college friends till then. I wasn't conservative or shy that way. I boozed, smoked and watched porn with roomies on mute while making deliberate dirty noises, but I had never been approached by any guy, nor had I approached anyone. I had some crushes in school, but I was more into staring at them from a distance rather than talking. I have forever been the average Indian girl with baby fat on her face and a slightly troubled metabolism. Though I have had boys call me cute, I have never been labelled as hot or a 'babe'. I don't think any of my classmates would have ever jerked off thinking about me. I was more of the girl-next-door-with-whom-you-could-share-your-dirty-thoughts-knowing-she-won't-tell-anyone type rather than the object of the dirty thoughts. And trust me, I was pretty happy with it. It was just that I didn't want Kiyan to see me the way every other boy saw me. I didn't want him to find me normal. I wanted to be special for him. But how could someone who was normal for everyone be special for anyone?

Royal Cafe was situated in the heart of Lucknow, Hazrat Ganj. I had this bad habit of calling my friends from a particular point, telling them I was on my way, and then watching them do stupid stuff while waiting for me. I did the same with Kiyan. I called him at a particular point near Sahu Cinema Hall and watched him from the other side of the road. Standing in front of a parked car with tinted glass, Kiyan kept checking his reflection. He was wearing a black shirt tucked inside his blue jeans and brown leather shoes. He had oiled and combed his otherwise-tousled hair into a decent right parting. He was looking unlike how he looked when I saw him the last two times; like a decent boy whom every girl would love to take home and introduce as her choice to her parents. After about three-four minutes of making him wait, I decided to present myself. I crossed the road. He smiled the moment he spotted me. I smiled back.

'Black suits you,' I said as he came up to me. For a few seconds, I thought he didn't know what I was referring to and then glancing at himself, realized it had to be his shirt.

'Thanks,' he said. His abrupt confused state was something I was beginning to like. I also noticed him looking at my kurti (or was it my figure?) I was in a sky-blue kurti with white flowers all over it and white jeggings below. My sandals had a block heel. I had put red paint on my nails and was smelling of lavender. I remember him telling me much later that there was nothing about me preventing him from proposing to me then and there. Though he didn't propose then, but to be honest, when I think back, I may have said yes.

'Here,' I said, stretching out my hand, which had a few notes in it.

'What's this?' he asked, genuinely surprised.

'I owed you money, remember? Isn't this why we are meeting?'

Is this really why we are meeting? I asked myself.

'But I told you the money belongs to all my friends. How can I take it?'

'Why don't you introduce me to your friends? I'll pay up individually then.'

Kiyan once again was lost in thought. And once again I enjoyed his confused expression. A boy would never introduce his girl to his friends before he proposed to her. Everyone suffers from basic insecurities, especially when it is about love. Love? Really? In a few meetings? What he said next made me think I was right.

'Since you are insisting so much, I'll take it,' Kiyan said, taking the notes.

'Good.' I so knew the introduce-me-to-your-friends ploy would work.

'I think we should go inside,' I said.

'Sure.'

Both of us entered the Royal Cafe. I liked the way he made way for me to enter first and followed behind. I like it when someone acts like a gentleman.

There weren't many people inside at the time. We took a table in the middle. I ordered an iced tea for myself while Kiyan asked for a cold coffee.

As the waiter took our order, we, for some time, just kept smiling at each other like fools without uttering a single word. I wanted him to initiate conversation this time. I wanted to see if he knew how to take charge. That's an important quality (a soul-arousing one at that!) in a man.

'These people won't shoot us if we talk,' he remarked. I sighed, thanking God silently that he had taken charge.

'If you say so,' I quipped.

'How is life?' he said.

'Life is what life should be like. Unpredictable. A few days ago, I didn't know you, and now here we are.'

'That's true, actually. Did you think about it?' It came out a tad more desperate than he would have liked. Or so I presumed.

'Think about what?'

'Our meeting at the ATM?'

'Obviously.' He flushed the moment I said it. 'I had to return the money to you.' This time, I intentionally teased him. The way I was manipulating his expressions were giving me a funny high.

'Oh!'

'I hope your girlfriend won't mind you meeting me here like this?' I asked. The most important thing before starting any journey—check if you have the ticket for it.

'No.'

My heart skipped a beat. A 'no' meant he had a girlfriend.

'Why not?'

'I don't have a girlfriend.'

Something within me calmed down.

'Why not? There are so many beautiful girls in your batch.' My teasing mode was on again. This time his face told me he understood.

'That's the problem, you see. With so many beautiful girls, how do you know who is the one for you? In fact, how does anyone know who is the one for you?'

I threw a sharp glance at him and said, 'I don't think you can decide the one for you and then meet the person. You meet the person and then know that he or she is the one for you.'

Kiyan kept looking at me. It was only when the waiter arrived with our order that he averted his eyes. Every second of that silence unfolded in me a certain part that I hadn't seen before. A part that thought someone could be more important to me than myself.

'What does your father do?' I asked, to break the romantic spell of silence that had consumed me and perhaps him too.

'He works for the PWD. And yours?'

'We have a garment shop in Aminabaad.'

'Nice.'

'So, what plans for Diwali? With friends?'

'Kind of. They will drink and smoke, which I am totally against.'

'Hmm, so am I.'

Kiyan darted an enquiring glance at me.

'Oh, I was only trying it in the train for a friend's sake. Casually, you know. Otherwise I don't.'

A smile of appreciation was duly flashed by Kiyan.

'If you keep away from your friends, then how do you party?'

'I don't. When I get time, I generally read books. Do you party a lot?'

'Not much. In Lucknow, it is mostly house parties. No good pub. In fact, no pub. There are mostly house parties, but those too are rare.'

'You sound sad, but you just said you don't party, so how does it matter if there's no pub.'

'I mean my friends keep asking me to parties, so I drop in once in a while when I'm here on holidays.'

The conversation came to a lull, during which Kiyan casually glanced around, looking at nothing in particular. I was sure he must be furiously thinking about what to say next. It was time to tell him something that I had been noticing for a while now but hadn't said a word about.

'Are you nervous?' I asked, looking directly at him.

'Am I nervous?'

'See? You are.'

'Why do you ask?' He had his eyebrows raised.

'Actually . . . you have been sipping my iced tea.'

Kiyan noticed his cold coffee sitting untouched on the table while he was halfway through the iced tea that I had ordered. Embarrassment was never so embarrassing.

I did have the cold coffee later, even though Kiyan insisted on ordering another iced tea for me. Our meeting lasted about thirty minutes, after which I took his leave as I had to visit one of my friends, Riti. We had to plan how to get my parents to let me attend the all-night party at Riti's boyfriend's bungalow in Gomti Nagar. Her boyfriend, Aman, had called all his friends for a post-Diwali alcohol party as his parents were out of town. After I met Riti, we cooked up a simple plan—I would get a call from her at around 9 p.m. on my landline, which I wouldn't pick up. Either my mother or father would. Riti would tell them she had fever and her parents were out of town, and request them to allow me to come over for the night. Sleepovers were a strict no-no for me and

51

hence this my-friend-needs-me story was important.

Everything went according to plan except that my favourite bua decided to visit us suddenly since I was there for the holidays. So, instead of 9 p.m., my dad dropped me off at Riti's place at around 10.45. Once dad left, after repeatedly asking Riti if she needed any medicine, which she refused, both Riti and I climbed into her father's Santro and drove to Aman's bungalow to find that the party had already begun.

'What took you so long, baby?' Aman asked as he opened the door for us.

'Sorry, baby. My friend was late,' Riti told him.

'Okay. No issues. Come in quickly.'

Once inside, Riti got busy with Aman. Most of the girls and boys at the party were Aman's friends whom I had not met. There were a few girls from college whom I knew, but they too were there with their boyfriends.

So I got myself a Budweiser. After a pint, my bladder was full. I asked the way to the washroom, which was attached to one of the bedrooms. When I came out after relieving myself, I couldn't believe my eyes.

Black Suits You

Right in front of me was Kiyan lying on the bed on his stomach, totally drunk.

And this guy, I wondered, had told me a few hours ago that he stayed away from alcohol. *Could this guy be even trusted?* I asked myself.

4

The next morning, Kiyan woke up with a bad hangover. He remembered the book event, the girl dancing on the bar top and also the way she had been adjusting the stiletto, but after that, nothing. How did he come to the hotel? Who brought him here? Was she the same girl who . . . He ordered some fresh lemon and heated up some water using the electric kettle in the room. It was while taking a shower that he realized he had a dark purple patch on his chest. A love bite. As he pressed it, he felt a slight twinge of pain. *When did this happen?* He wondered and tried to think hard about what all had happened the night before. All he could remember was talking to the girl who had danced atop the bar. She had a problem with her stilettos and then . . . all blank. Storming out of the shower with water dripping down his naked body, Kiyan called up the reception.

'Sir, someone left you with our security guard at the gate. We took you to your room,' the receptionist said in answer to Kiyan's query.

'Left me, as in?'

'You were . . .' the receptionist took time to choose his words wisely. It was a corporate booking guest he was talking to. He didn't want to upset him.

'I believe you drank a little more than usual, so you were not able to walk or even talk.'

'Hmm, okay.' Kiyan had understood by now that it was the girl. She must have spiked his drink to . . . give him a love bite? Or did they sleep together, and he didn't remember anything? He once again pressed the bite mark to feel the pain. What did she want? This wasn't fan-like behaviour, he thought, and turned to go back to the washroom when the phone rang. Kiyan was quick to pick up.

'Hello, mister bestselling author,' A female voice said. It was a confident, honey-dipped girly voice.

'Who is this?' Kiyan tried to look for but didn't find any caller ID facility on the hotel room phone.

'You were with me last night,' she said with a hint of amusement. It wasn't a surprise for Kiyan.

'What does the bite mark mean?'

'I wanted to tell you a lot of things, Kiyan. But words failed me. So, I thought of expressing them through the bite.'

Her words proved Kiyan wasn't talking to someone dumb. He took his time to speak.

'What happened, mister bestselling author? You too at a loss of words like me? You too want to express it differently?' She giggled. Her giggle had an alluring quality to it. He would never forget it, Kiyan knew.

'What is all this about, if I may know,' Kiyan said.

'No, you may not.'

'What?'

'You said if . . . so I said no, you can't.'

Kiyan was about to frame something sterner when he heard her giggle again.

'I'm kidding, mister bestselling author,' she said. Kiyan was yet to understand if the 'mister bestselling author' was a taunt or otherwise. It disturbed him slightly.

'Call me Kiyan.'

'I will . . . when our breaths fall on each other's faces . . . I surely will.'

'And what do I call you?'

'Call me Kashti,' she said.

'Kashti . . .' Kiyan repeated under his breath.

'That was orgasmic,' Kashti said with a sigh.

'What do you want Kashti? Why have you been following me to every book event?'

'That accusatory tone is making me feel guilty, mister bestselling author.'

'I just asked a simple question—what do you want?'

'Okay. I want to fuck you. How about that?'

Kiyan found her bluntness unsettling.

'I don't go around fucking my fans.'

'Now you are being presumptuous, mister bestselling author.'

'Why would you say that?'

'That's because I never said I am your fan.'

If this had been a novel then Kiyan knew this was the moment when the plot thickened.

'Then who are you?'

'What's the rush?'

'So you are going to tell me some day?'

'Else I wouldn't have approached you.'

'You have sent stalker-ish photographs, a note and given me a love bite. That's not exactly approaching someone.'

'Are you ruing the fact that I haven't approached you yet?'

This was a trick question. What should he say? A direct yes? Because that was the truth. He wanted to know who this girl was who had given him the deepest love bite of his life, someone he wrongly thought was a fan and one whose name—Kashti—made him feel as if he had heard it somewhere, though he wasn't sure where.

'What if I say yes?' Kiyan said.

'You say *if* a lot, mister bestselling author. Girls fall for guys who are specific with their intentions. Care to be confident for a change?'

Girls fall for guys . . . there was intention hidden in the subtext of it, Kiyan thought and then warned himself not to be presumptuous about it.

'Okay, I'll be specific. Meet me,' he said.

A pause later, Kashti said, 'Very soon.' And cut the line. Kiyan immediately called the reception and asked if the call could be traced to the number it was made from. The receptionist took half a minute and said the call was made from room no. 717, in the same hotel where he was. Kiyan turned around quickly but stopped when he noticed himself in the full-length mirror. He was naked. And he hadn't realized it earlier, but the conversation had given him a major hard-on.

He quickly dressed to scoot to room no. 717, which was a floor above the one he was in. The door was open when he reached. He knocked once and then stepped in, alert. The bed was messy, the curtains were drawn and a tea set was on the centre table. He could see someone had just finished the tea in one of the cups. Kiyan was taken aback when a housekeeping boy came out of the washroom.

'Yes sir, may I help you?'

'Where's the guest you had in this room?'

'She just checked out.'

Kiyan rushed downstairs, but he was too late. The guest, as he was told by the receptionist, had checked out of the hotel half an hour ago but had gone back to the room on the pretext of looking for her phone. *And that's when she called me*, Kiyan thought. With much persuasion and by using his charm, Kiyan was shown her name but not the address. Her name indeed was Kashti. But there wasn't any surname. He knew he had no option but to wait for her to get in touch with him again.

* * *

That didn't happen for an entire week. It had become a pattern now—she would appear during the book event and then disappear for the entire week. The following weekend, it was time for another book event, this time in Mumbai.

During the three-hour-long launch in Crossword, Kemps Corner, Kiyan's eyes were working hard, searching for her. *One glimpse. That's all I'll need to recognize the girl this time.* Or that's what he kept telling himself, knowing well that he didn't remember much about Kashti except that she danced like crazy and had fiddled with her stilettos. And of course, that she was daring enough to spike his drink and take advantage of him. He knew she had to be there and had a gut feeling she must be seeking an opportunity to surprise him. And that made him remain alert.

Compared with other cities, the queue for book signing was the longest in Mumbai. It took him close to two hours to only sign the books and pose for selfies with the readers. By the time the event ended, the entire stock of the trilogy at the store had been sold out. This time, his editor Natasha and marketing manager Supriya were present at the launch. They decided to go to Social in Colaba for dinner.

Kiyan tried hard but couldn't focus on the discussion. He kept fidgeting with his phone, looking around, and sipping his wine a little too frequently.

'Are you okay?' Natasha enquired, sensing his restlessness.

'Yeah, yeah. A little tired.'

'I know. The constant weekend travel can be tiresome. But it's all for the books. A couple more cities and then you shall be grounded till you give us your next bestseller,' Natasha said.

Kiyan was amused at the way Natasha kept passive aggressively reminding him of the next book.

'I shared the one line you messaged me the other day with my sales team,' Natasha said. 'They loved it. So go ahead and give me a manuscript soon.'

'Even I loved it,' Supriya said. 'I had an interesting marketing pitch for it as well. We would tell people it happened for real to you. I'm sure it would then have that extra wow factor. What say?'

'That would be perfect!' Natasha quipped.

Kiyan gave them a wry smile. Only he knew what he was going through. Just then, the waiter came to their table, and Natasha got busy ordering the main course. Kiyan noticed his phone was ringing, with an unknown number flashing on the screen. The moment it turned into a missed call, Kiyan checked the number on Truecaller. It was listed as 'KR'. His brow creased on reading his own initials. It struck him that 'KR' in

Bengali could be read as 'Kay Are', as in 'who else?' If it was intentional word play, Kiyan was impressed. This girl—Kashti—was irksome and impressive at the same time. He hadn't come across this combination before.

His phone rang again. This time, Kiyan excused himself and walked towards the restroom. Standing outside, he took the call.

'Kashti?' he said.

'Commendable, mister bestselling author. I like the fact that you took the trouble of finding out whose number it was.'

'Hard work never runs out of fashion after all,' Kiyan said.

'Never. Like my hard work is still there on your chest,' she giggled. Kiyan felt a desperate urge to see her face right at that moment. Like most creative people, Kiyan too would get impatient when something he sought eluded him. Nothing could calm his restlessness when it came to unveiling something.

'What did you decide about meeting me?' Kiyan asked.

'Someone's sounding desperate to meet.'

'I'm not the one who left a bite mark.'

'Uh-huh. All right, mister bestselling author. I'll meet you tonight.'

Kiyan felt a stirring in his loins.

* * *

A Girl's Diary

27th February 2016, 11:48 PM.

I stood by the bed, staring at Kiyan. He was wearing the same clothes that he had on when he had met me earlier in the day. Only his shirt was no longer tucked into his jeans and the sleeves were rolled up. He was mumbling something. I didn't like the sight. Till now, he had led me to believe he was different from others. Was that all false? I bent down slightly to make sense of his inebriated mumbling but still couldn't understand anything. I sat beside him and leaned forward with my ears close to his mouth.

He drawled on my name.

It was obvious he hadn't seen me, for his eyes were closed and yet he was murmuring my name.

'What is it Kiyan?' I whispered.

Kiyan tried opening his eyes. It took him 2-3 attempts. The way he kept squinting, trying to make out who it was in front of him, told me his vision must be blurred. He once again said my name and then said,

'I love you.'

I kept looking at him, not saying a word. Did he really mean what he said? He was sloshed. When someone is sloshed, they either speak shit or the truth. I was lost in my thoughts when Kiyan surprised me by reaching out for and holding my hand rather tightly. Using it as support, he sat up on the bed.

'Everything about her is beautiful,' he said, placing his hands on my shoulder in a you-are-my-buddy manner.

'You know it when you see something perfect . . .'

'How do you know she is perfect?' I cut him short.

Kiyan made a disgusted face as if he didn't like the interruption. He brought a finger to his lips and gestured for me to keep quiet.

'I know she is. As I was saying, when you see someone that perfect, you start hating your own imperfections simply because you know you don't deserve that perfect someone. And you start behaving like what you are not just to win them. I lied to her today that I don't drink. I lied to her in the train that I don't smoke. The only thing I didn't lie to her about was that I indeed am single. But you tell me, how do I deserve the perfection that she is?'

Though he was drunk I knew he was indeed repentant about his lies. The anguish in his voice told me he could possibly even be in love with me, though I do not believe someone can fall in love without thoroughly knowing the other person.

'By giving her so much respect, you already deserve her, Kiyan,' I said.

He turned to give me a you-kidding-me look. I maintained a serious face to show him I meant what I had said. When I didn't waver, Kiyan swallowed a lump.

'Are you sure?'

'I'm dead sure. You sleep now.' I helped him lie down once again. Throughout, our eyes remained linked. At that moment, he didn't realize who I was but I did realize who he really was. Kiyan closed his eyes while I spent the night sitting on the bed right beside him. In the wee hours of dawn, when I returned home, I had made a decision.

Our romance became the talk of the college simply because we were the only IT-Mechanical couple. Kiyan graduated one year before I did.

I now think the single most difficult thing to find after God is the right person for oneself. I was glad I didn't have to seek Kiyan and that the universe brought us together, in rather filmy style. Every day with him felt like a blessing. And the more I thought it was a blessing, the more I got scared because I knew life never remains the same. Everything is a cycle. Sooner or later, the wheels turn.

Our smooth relationship hit the first speed breaker after Kiyan graduated from college. Neither of us saw it coming. Now that I think back, I believe speed breakers are important for relationships. They give you reason to check if what you have is really a relationship or an illusion of a relationship. They help you see the relationship in an objective manner, washing off the blind spots.

Kiyan got a job in an automobile MNC in Gurgaon after college. He shifted there and lived with a couple of other guys in a rented flat. Suddenly, the good times seemed far away. All we could do was either talk to each other on the phone or see each other over video calls. Nothing could substitute the time we had spent together. Every fortnight, Kiyan used to catch a train from New Delhi to Chandigarh and then take a bus to Wakhnaghat only to meet me. I knew it was taxing on him, but I was also glad he chose to do it for our sake. This great romantic gesture floored me, but what I didn't know was that Kiyan was doing it out of insecurity. Every time I told him I was going out with friends, the first question would be 'How many guys will be there?' Every time I, only casually, talked about a male friend, Kiyan would come to college the following weekend. He also never missed a chance to take me to a family function of his. He did so not only because he wanted to introduce me to his family, but also to make me more and more invested in the relationship. I couldn't digest the deliberateness of it. I desperately wanted to see it as his way of consolidating our commitment, but the truth was it was his way of emotionally imprisoning me so that I never left him. He thought if I knew his family, it would be yet another factor to consider if I ever decided to leave him. It was a psychological investment that he was compelling me to make. I didn't complain because I loved him. I only hoped he understood the intensity of my love towards him, and that there was no need for such emotional or psychological tactics or back-up plans. I'm sure he too didn't like it himself, but perhaps his insecurity was so strong that he couldn't control himself.

Things went on like this for six months, and I was fine with it, but when he asked me for my email and my social networking passwords, I flared up.

'What do you need my passwords for?' I asked him over the phone.

'I only want to see who all you talk to.'

'Or you want to see who all I flirt with?'

'Do you?'

'I won't answer that.'

'That means you do.' Kiyan's pent-up fears came out in a shout. 'How could you? We've been in a relationship for the past three years now!'

'That's my point too. It has been three years. How could you suspect me, Kiyan? I have never even thought of another guy, forget about flirting with someone.'

'Really? Then why do you have a problem sharing your passwords. I don't have a problem sharing mine. Loveforever654 is my password for all my accounts. You can check,' he said.

'I don't need your password, Kiyan. I don't want to check. I trust you. And thought you trusted me too.'

'Maybe that's because you know I'm not big on social networking.'

'Shut up.'

'Okay, I trust you as well. I really do, but I want to check too. Why should it be an issue if I want to check your email? I'm your boyfriend after all.'

'Being your girlfriend doesn't mean I'm not entitled to any private space. We aren't each other's purchased goods, for God's sake!'

'Why don't you tell me up front? You have someone better than me. That you are done with me.'

There was a pause after which I shouted back, 'I can't believe you just said that, Kiyan.' I was in tears as I disconnected the phone line. Kiyan tried calling back a few times, but I didn't pick up. What's ego to a man is hurt to a woman. Ego didn't allow Kiyan to pursue me again while hurt didn't let me reach out to him, even though deep in our hearts our love was tormenting us. I deleted his number on my mobile phone and each blocked the other on their social networking profiles. But what we could never do was learn to live without each other. For the first time, we understood the sharp edges of love and how they can injure if one doesn't take care of the relationship. Now I know that a relationship isn't formed by two perfect beings. It's formed by ordinary people with normal fears and traits but with a will to understand the other and a respect for the other's point of view. If that will and respect don't exist, then nothing can make up for the hollowness that will invariably develop over time.

Six months later, I too got a job in an IT MNC in Gurgaon. There was a gap of three months before I graduated and could join. On my second day at work, I got an email on my office ID from Kiyan.

Congrats on the job. Can we please meet?

At first, I thought I wouldn't reply. But that night, I realized I had spent too many good moments with him to not agree to this one request of his. Most importantly, somewhere, I too wanted to meet him. We had broken off the relationship without any closure. I thought perhaps the meeting would give our story the kind of closure it needed for us to actually move on in our lives.

We met at a coffee shop in Ambience Mall in Gurgaon. Kiyan had gained weight and his eyes seemed puffy. It was evident he was drinking a lot. Anyone could tell from his appearance that something was seriously wrong. I was on the verge of tears at seeing him like this but somehow managed to hold them back.

'What has happened to you, Kiyan?'

'My father was in the ICU a month ago. He had an ulcer in his stomach that burst. The doctors gave him forty-eight hours to live. Everyone was in the hospital. So was I. At night, I was asked to go home and rest by the elders in the family. I refused, but then I was forcibly made to go home. When in the dead of the night I went to my balcony and stared at the moon, the beauty of it made me realize the ugly truth of life. What if Dad didn't open his eyes the next morning? I can't tell you how I felt. Like a loser. A defeated person. An insignificant speck of dust. I wanted to hug someone and cry. I realized then that one is lucky to have someone to share your smiles with but blessed only if you have a shoulder to cry on. I missed you, like I have never missed you before. The void that was created after we broke up stared me right in my face, scaring me, disturbing me, shaking me to my core. That moment made me realize your real worth in my life. I don't want to lose you. Can you please forgive me for however I may have hurt you? And can we please start again?'

He tried to grasp my hands as he finished. I let him.

There was a moment of silence. I blinked once and tears rolled out of my eyes. I stood up. Kiyan too stood up in reflex. I embraced him as tightly as I could. Going by what Kiyan had told me, it was my turn to feel blessed because I was crying and had a shoulder to rely on.

71

5

Bengaluru
5 March 2016
Saturday, 9.45 p.m.

It had been a bluff. Kiyan had waited for Kashti to approach him, to meet him during dinner, after dinner and even when he was about to check out of the hotel the next morning, but it didn't happen. He tried her number several times, but it remained switched off. He sent her several messages before checking out, but they were yet to be delivered. On his flight back home, a girl had casually asked him about a particular seat number and he had thought it was Kashti. He could lie to the whole world, but he couldn't lie to himself. Kashti had indeed left an indelible mark; literally on his chest and otherwise too. Earlier, if he had only vaguely been considering turning the girl who had danced on the bar top in Pune into a character in his next novel, then he was now sure she would feature in his next story. And for the story's sake, he hoped Kashti would meet him again. At least once.

As usual, there was no communication from Kashti for the entire week. His ego—since *he* was the author—didn't allow him to digest the fact that he was perturbed by a mere fan. Of course, she had said she wasn't one, but Kiyan was smart enough to understand it was one of those psychological ploys to stand out amid the crowd. He tried calling up Kashti from a couple of other numbers so that he didn't come across as obvious or desperate, but the number was switched off all the through the week. By the time it was next weekend, time for the event in Bengaluru, Kiyan was hoping against hope for Kashti to get in touch with him, like she had been doing for the last few times . . . during, just before or right after the book events.

Never before had it happened that a girl had given him such a painful hickey and he knew nothing about her. He was denying it internally, but it had turned into a duel of sorts where she was clearly winning, and his male ego wasn't ready to take it. The first time, he hadn't given a damn, the second time he had been curious, but from the third instance, she had become an unwilling obsession. Maybe it was because he couldn't understand her yet. Or maybe it was so because he wanted to know her. She may say otherwise, Kiyan told himself, but she was indeed a fan. Who else could she be?

Two hours after checking in at The Park in Bengaluru, Kiyan decided to sweat it out at the gym. He worked on his abs, thighs and butt, and did an hour of cardio before deciding he had done enough. While leaving the gym, the in-house trainer came to him and asked if he would like to use their newly renovated steam room.

'Today it is for free, sir,' the trainer said.

Kiyan had ample time to kill till the book event in the evening, and a little steam sounded like a good idea. 'Sure.'

'I'll get the room ready,' the trainer said and scooted off. Kiyan waited, looking around and tapping his foot to a peppy number playing on the speakers. There were only three more people in the gym; two ladies and one guy. All three were foreigners. The trainer came back and led Kiyan to the steam room.

'You can keep your clothes and shoes here, sir,' the trainer said, pointing at a locker.

'Sure, thanks,' Kiyan said and stripped off his T-shirt, tracksuit trouser and shoes. The trainer gave him a white towel that he wrapped around his waist and then took off his briefs as well.

'Sir, sit inside and the steam will start soon.'

'Sure.'

'Do you want me to play any particular song?'

'Anything by Enrique?'

'Sure, sir.'

As Kiyan entered the steam room, he realized he was alone. The waterproof speakers all around the room started buzzing with Enrique's number *Somebody's Me*.

Kiyan sat down on one of the wooden benches, bending slightly forward, keeping his elbows on his knees and resting his face on his palms. His foot tapped in time to the music as steam flooded the room. A good three minutes later, when Kiyan's body broke out into a sweat, the music suddenly switched to *Fade into You*. Kiyan had heard the song before. It was by Mazzy Star. Suddenly, he heard the door unlock and then lock again. He felt someone sitting beside him but didn't care to look up. Not until he felt something thrown at him. Kiyan stood up with a start and realized it was a towel. He tried to look but there was too much steam in the room to see through it clearly. Kiyan turned to move towards the door when he felt a hand on his waist. Right where he had tucked in the loose end of his towel.

'What's the hurry, mister bestselling author?' Kashti said. And tugged at the loose end of the towel. It fell to the ground. Kiyan could still not see her clearly. It was a vague image, just like the memory of the pub in Pune. He felt her hand cup his balls, which had contracted by then. He swallowed a lump in his throat. How could their first proper meeting be this sexy? What kind of girl would be this bold, except, of course, if she had walked right out of his erotic trilogy? The thought gave Kiyan a different kind of high. He felt her hand squeezing his balls with the base of her palm. He stretched out his hands to feel her. And ended up touching her firm breasts. He withdrew his hands quickly, not wanting to offend her.

'You are Kashti, right?' he said and felt like a fool to state the obvious.

'Why, do you want me to be someone else?' Her fingers were touching the base of his hard shaft. With the other hand she grabbed one of his wrists and brought his hand close to her face. She started licking the lines on his palm. It tickled him in an arousing way.

'What are you doing?'

'I'm putting myself on your destiny line,' she said.

Kiyan resisted the urge but knew he was growing down there every second. Not able to withstand the tickle, he pushed Kashti and pinned her against the wall. Her body was slippery with sweat, while her face was only slightly visible to him now.

'Why did you drug and bite me?'

'What do you think?' She was trying to fight him, but Kiyan had her hands pinned strongly.

'Answer me.'

She stepped on his feet. And came close to his face.

'I wanted to taste you, mister bestselling author.'

Though there was a lot of steam between them, he knew she was staring at him just like he was at her. Kiyan went for her lips. She moved her face. He sucked her ear lobes instead. And as she slowly moved her face towards him, rubbing her cheeks against his lips, her quivering lips finally met his. And a devouring game began. Kiyan let go of her hands. He cupped her face while placing her hands on his outer thighs. Her nails dug deep into his flesh. The erotic music, the steam, the nudity and the fact that they couldn't see each other clearly turned on both of them. They were like two animals, primal and pure. And since it was instinctive, they were sucked into the moment more than they would have otherwise. Kiyan's hands slid down to her waist while she grabbed his hard dick, this time with just the kind of pressure that made him shut his eyes. Kashti kept up the steady pace with her hand, imagining his facial expressions by his soft grunts. He broke the smooch.

'This isn't real, this can't be real,' Kiyan whispered, feeling the orgasm build up inside him.

'Only when this is over will you realize how real it was,' she said, as Kiyan let out a low moan.

'Was it only this you wanted?' he asked.

'This . . . you wanted, Kiyan. You wanted to meet.'

'And what do you want?' he asked, grunting softly.

In response, she increased the pace of her hand. His grunts turned louder, and finally Kiyan sprayed his seed in three full bursts.

'Patience, mister bestselling author,' Kashti said. Kiyan was busy catching his breath while opening his eyes slowly. Her hand was no longer on his penis. As the passion subsided, Kiyan felt embarrassed. Never before had a girl led him so easily into a sexual encounter. This girl had something about her.

'Look, I don't do this kind of thing and . . .' The steam in the room had reduced. There was nobody in the room. He heard a knock. The trainer peeped in.

'Sir, did you enjoy it? Would you like to continue?'

Kiyan rushed for his towel and asked, 'Where is the girl?'

'Which girl, sir?'

'The one who was with me in this room.'

'There was a girl? I'm sorry, I didn't see anyone.'

The song inside changed to *Rub You the Right Way* by Johnny Gill. The lyrics amused him as he walked out of the steam room. She had kept her promise. She had met him. But would she meet him again? The way people meet, not animals, he wondered. As he reached his locker, there was a Post-it note stuck to it.

1 minute and 13 seconds. Mister bestselling author, I hope you will last longer next time. ☺

Kiyan smiled and tore the note into pieces. Now he knew there would be a next time.

* * *

A GIRL'S DIARY

5 March 2016, 10.40 p.m.

Loving someone is one thing. Living with that person is another thing completely. Kiyan may be a bestselling author now, and

I'm sure there will be girls and women dying to make him theirs in every sense of the word, but what is their fantasy was actually my reality. I lived with him.

I was happy our love story was back on track again. This time permanently. We both had our offices in Gurgaon and both our places were twenty minutes from our offices. He lived in wing A with another guy while I lived in wing B of the same society with two more girls. Weekdays simply flew by in a monotonous loop, and it was only during weekends that we could give time to our relationship, to us. Kiyan's roommate used to travel to his hometown in Jaipur every Friday night, leaving the entire flat to us. And we lived together throughout the weekend. Living with him, I realized Kiyan and I were two different human beings when it came to sex.

I have never heard this from friends or heard this discussed anywhere, but that Saturday night when Kiyan and I had sex for the first time, I realized two people who are genuinely in love can be strangers sexually as well. I'm not talking about sexual compatibility. I'm talking about sexual preferences. It was the first time I ever had sex, and I remember we hadn't planned it. Like any other weekend, we had come back from watching a movie and trying a new restaurant nearby for dinner. It wasn't that he had touched or kissed me for the first time that night, but when I was changing in the darkness of his bedroom I noticed him standing by the door. Usually, Kiyan would give me enough space and never made me feel conscious, but seeing him stand by the door, I knew this would be a night we, at least I, would remember for years to come. But it wasn't just the moment I remember, but the way it all happened. He rushed to me when I doffed my T-shirt and wasted no time in undressing me completely. I wanted him to go slow and take his time. I was his anyway, but he was in a hurry as if I was going to slip away from him. I tried to explain this to him, but he seemed possessed with lust. I knew he loved me, but I was disturbed by the way he seemed to devour me. I wanted him to go slow, but he was all over me. He bit me, pinched me and even spanked me. I almost felt like crying but didn't. It was the only time I thought I didn't know the person I was in love with. It's not that we hadn't discussed sex till then. We had. We had made out in college too, but he was never this aggressive. It wasn't his aggression that was upsetting me. I wasn't averse to consensual aggression in bed, but I also wanted to take it slow. When the same thing happened the following 3-4 weekends, I realized it was a pattern. I understood that he would give only his way of lovemaking a priority. I tried to talk to Kiyan about it, and he would agree we would take it slow, but the moment we would begin, his way of lovemaking would take precedence. He would satisfy all his kinks and I felt like the object of his sexual urges rather than an equal partner in the act. He wasn't harming me and yet he was. He wasn't humiliating me and yet he was. He wasn't intentionally pushing me to feel uncomfortable with him and yet he was. This was one thing that started affecting me. However, it didn't affect our relationship. I learnt that love also meant internalising something and keeping it locked away all to yourself to safeguard your relationship. It's funny how a relationship is about two people, but when it comes to safeguard it, more often than not it becomes one person's prerogative.

After a point, I couldn't talk to him about it, fearing it would somewhere ruin our relationship if he didn't understand

what my point was. I discussed it with a
close friend of mine, Shriya, and she too
said the same thing. It's rare that a guy
would understand your point of view when
it came to sexuality. They are too weighed
down by their own urges. I was happy I
didn't let this 'in-bed' issue affect
what I shared with Kiyan when I wasn't
in bed with him. But I was a little hurt
that he didn't understand it himself. I
realize that I didn't give him hints but
the person you love should understand you
without hints, right? It's like anyone
would understand a film with subtitles,
but someone in love with the film would
go the distance and perhaps learn the
language to understand it like a native.
With time, I accepted this dissimilarity
between the two of us. And somewhere, my
own sexual preferences blurred as I gave
in to his. If relationships were soaps,
then sex was at best the scent of it. The
lather of course had to be love. And Kiyan
and I had more than enough lather.

Five months after I lost my virginity
to Kiyan, his roommate shifted base to
Bangalore. Kiyan suggested it would be
better if we lived together. That way,
our expenses would be curtailed to an
extent, and we could live as a couple. At

this point, I asked him if we could get
married. Kiyan said he wasn't ready yet.
When that was his response, I felt it
was yet another addition to the list of
situations wherein I was giving in to his
preferences. Shriya told me this giving in
was the start of the end, since it turns
people into what they are not. And though
you fall in love with someone by being
who you really are, you can't sustain the
love by being what you are not. Sooner or
later, it chokes the relationship to a
slow death. I didn't believe her because
I was sure mine wouldn't die out. Ours
wouldn't die out.

6

Smaller cities have a charm of their own. The people, the roads, the shops, the cows, the beggars, the out-of-order street lights, the wannabe malls—everything seems to tell you something. A story. Everything and everyone seems to reach out to you, wanting to form a relationship. *Like they haven't had a patient listener for a long time*, Kiyan wondered as his chauffeur drove him from the airport to Lemon Tree Hotel.

The small and vibrant city of Indore seemed to create a sense of déjà vu in him, with its lanes and by-lanes that had some similarity to the lanes of his home town, Lucknow. Also, it was time for yet another book event. *Yet another meeting with Kashti?* he wondered. Kiyan couldn't believe she had jerked him off the last time they had met. It wasn't really a meeting. It was barging into his private space. But thinking about the way she had done it still aroused him. He was yet to meet a girl like that. Fandom is one thing but to go ahead and jerk off your favourite author, that too in a steam room, was adventurous. Though she had clarified she wasn't a fan, Kiyan couldn't think who else she could be. Perhaps the whole I-am-not-your-fan thing was a ploy to raise his curiosity about her further. Getting involved—in whatever scope—with one's reader was a cardinal sin if his marketing team was to be believed. Involvement broke the myth, it demystified the creator, it made him accessible and once someone was accessible, they became ordinary. If gods were found on every corner of streets, every hour, then people wouldn't have found religion a worthy enough pursuit. But Kiyan had not only allowed Kashti to approach him, he had also let her lead him to his most vulnerable moment. Would she care to continue pursuing him? Kiyan checked in to the hotel, feeling slightly upset with himself for the first time after the steam room incident last week. *Was he really that easy?* Stalk him for a few book events, intrigue him and voila, you can jerk him off. He would act snobbish if she approached him again in Indore. 'If' and 'she' being the keywords. If she didn't, then it would prove that he indeed was easy. He felt all the more stupid because he had met Kashti twice by now—once in the pub in Pune and then in the steam room in Bangalore—but still didn't know exactly how she looked. And that was the most arousing part of whatever he shared with her—to be so intimate with someone you haven't really seen. So when he tried to think of her, she could be anyone. This reality had the recipe for the perfect fantasy. And perfect fantasies, unlike perfect crime, can actually be perfect.

The landline in the hotel room rang twice after he checked in. And both the times, the hurry in his gait to pick up disappointed him. *I shouldn't be this eager.* What was worse was the double disappointment he felt after he picked up the phone and realized it wasn't Kashti. *When will we meet again?* If someone makes you expect things in their absence, then they are definitely controlling you. Controlling *the* Kiyan Roy. He smirked and promised himself he wouldn't think about Kashti again even if she approached him in Indore.

The crowd at the Indore book event was the quietest he had witnessed. Kiyan had noticed over subsequent book events that people in smaller towns were slightly more hesitant in putting forward their queries than they were in the metros. Even the age group of the audience seemed a little over his normal target audience. And most of the younger ones had come with their parents or some guardian. It was while he was signing the books that Kiyan realized that most of the older members of the audience had come in seeing the hoopla in the bookstore. They didn't know much about the books he had written but wanted to be a part of the crowd. It amused Kiyan, and he was happy to sign the trilogy for them, knowing well the reaction would be extreme from the fifty-plus readers if they read his erotica trilogy. Either they would abuse him, stating he was destroying Indian culture, or bless him for rekindling the lust that was fighting a hopeless battle against age within them. The surprise of the event, however, was when a particular guy of Kiyan's age came up and requested an autograph. When Kiyan looked up at him to inquire his name he realized he was staring at his once-upon-a-time school friend.

'What the fuck! Mridul?' Kiyan stood up.

'So the big author still recognizes small friends,' Mridul said jocularly and reciprocated Kiyan's hug.

'Just wait for me. Let me finish signing the books. We'll catch up.'

'Sure,' Mridul said and stood aside while Kiyan started signing the books fast. Memories of Mridul and him in school flooded back. They were best friends once. They had lost touch once college began. Mridul went to study in VIT, Vellore, while Kiyan was in a college near Shimla. And now seeing Mridul, he didn't know what had made him happy—the sight of an old friend or the memories that it had triggered.

Right after the book signing, selfies and talking to a few readers, Kiyan finally excused himself and left with Mridul. They located a CCD outlet nearby and sat down over a hot cappuccino. Kiyan learnt Mridul's wife was from Indore and that he had happened to learn about the book event when he had read an article about it in the morning.

'You know, I searched a lot for you on social media. Then I found your page, but realized it is not you who is running it.'

'All my social accounts are handled by my publisher's marketing team.'

'Bade log, badi baatein,' Mridul said teasingly.

'Come on! Fame is a part of the profession.'

'I know. I was kidding,' Mridul said. He sipped some coffee and then added, 'You remember Debi?'

Of course he remembered Debi, his first crush, first love and first heartbreak. When too many firsts happen to be the same person, it probably means you were a kid for too long.

'What about her?'

'She is a mother of two now! Can you beat that?'

'Well, had I been her husband, I would've subjected her to the same fate as well,' Kiyan said and winked at Mridul. Both laughed.

'What's your relationship status? Marriage on the cards anytime soon?'

'Not really. Fame has just touched me. My publishers want me to keep my desirability quotient high.'

'And being single helps?'

'It does. Or so they say. Especially, if you write romance or erotica, as people fall for the mind that creates it.'

'I get that.'

After an almost two-hour-long chat, Mridul suggested they check out Chappan Dukan and Sarafa Bazaar for their food. These two destinations in Indore were like what Taj is for Agra. When they reached, Kiyan couldn't believe the number of people hovering inside and outside the Chappan shops. Mridul told him 90 per cent were locals who could never get enough of either Chappan or Sarafa. Both friends ate from different shops and then headed towards Sarafa.

Sarafa Bazaar was a jewellery hotspot during the day and a foodie's heaven at night. It reminded him of his hometown Lucknow, where food had an important place in everyday life. While eating faluda from one of the Sarafa shops, Kiyan received a call. It was from an unknown number so he decided to avoid it. The moment his phone stopped ringing the Truecaller app displayed the name of the caller as 'KR'. Kiyan immediately looked around for a possible stalker.

'What happened?' Mridul asked.

Kiyan was alert now. His phone rang again. It was the same number, but not unknown any more even though it was displaying only digits. Kiyan picked up. He was embarrassed to hear what was playing on the other side. It was him moaning Kashti's name. A moment later, the recording ended and Kashti came on line with a giggle. Hearing her voice, Kiyan knew he had actually missed her.

'How are you, mister bestselling author? All good?' Kashti asked, controlling her giggle. There was a slight arrogance that Kiyan sensed. *Who the fuck did she think she was,* he thought and said aloud, 'I'm with a friend right now. Can you call me later?'

'I can see that,' Kashti said. It was enough for Kiyan to stop talking and look around again. He knew Mridul was giving him looks, but he didn't care.

'It feels so wonderful to control someone. Especially if he is some celeb,' she said and giggled once again.

'So, it's a bluff. You aren't nearby,' he said.

'You are wearing a beige cotton shirt with black trousers, were eating Bhutte-Ka-Kiss a minute ago and are now having faluda. Yes, it was a bluff.' The giggle was back. And this time the giggle had a taunt. Kiyan cut the line.

'Mridul, something has come up. I think I will head back to my hotel,' he told his friend.

'Are you sure?'

'Yes. It was nice catching up. Let's not lose touch again.'

They exchanged numbers. Though Mridul tried to invite him home, Kiyan had a plan in mind, and he knew it was more important to execute it. What happened the moment he left Mridul was exactly what he had anticipated. His phone rang, flashing Kashti's number.

'Yes?' he said, walking amid the crowd at Sarafa.

'Angry with me, mister bestselling author?'

'Is this wild goose chase necessary? Especially after what happened last time?'

'It seems what happened last time has remained with you.'

'Hasn't it remained with you?'

'You know it has.'

'Let's come straight to the point. Why are you not meeting me?' he asked, making himself comfortable under a lamp whose light was off. There was a small dark patch where he stood against a shuttered jewellery shop. There were no eateries nearby.

'I believe the moment two people meet, their story starts heading towards an ending. I don't want the beginning of that end to start,' she said.

Interesting, thought Kiyan. He made a mental note to use the quote in his next book and then said, 'That way nothing will ever begin.'

'I know. It's paradoxical, but it is a problem nevertheless. I want to live out this phase as long as possible, because trust me, this is the best part of a relationship—when it has not begun, but in your mind it already has.'

'Relationship?'

'Relationship.'

'Hmm. But then what's the solution? My last book event is next week in Goa.'

'What are you hinting at, mister bestselling author?'

'Nothing. I'm only asking.'

'Do you really know me enough to ask me what you asked?'

'I want to.'

'Maybe you already know me.'

'Are you this cryptic with everyone, or is it just me?'

'I don't jerk off everyone in steam rooms, mister bestselling author.'

'So, it's only me.'

'Only you.'

'Why? You said you aren't even a fan.'

'Why, is it necessary to be a fan to be interested in you?'

'My gut says not to believe you on this.'

'What else does your gut say?'

'I want to meet you.'

'Are you seeking a story in me, mister bestselling author?'

'Maybe. Maybe not.' Kiyan smirked. It was his chance to be cryptic.

'It's a trap, isn't it?'

'Why don't you discover it yourself?'

'By meeting you?'

'Hmm.'

There was silence. Kiyan was hoping she would say yes while Kashti only breathed gently into the phone.

'We'll meet in Goa,' she said.

'Not in a steam room, I hope.'

There was a hint of a giggle.

'By the beach,' she specified.

'I'll wait.'

'Kiyan . . . I have a gift for you.'

This was the first time she had said his name. And it sounded acutely sexy.

'What is it?'

'There are some things that can only burn, but not dissolve into ashes. My passion for you is one such thing.'

Was that line a gift? Before Kiyan could say anything, she hung up. And by now he knew it was futile to get in touch with her. Not till he was in Goa the next weekend.

* * *

A Girl's Diary

13 March 2016
Sunday, 10 a.m.

I remember the day clearly. Why wouldn't I? It was a day when our relationship took a major turn. An unexpected turn. I had a sudden client call in office because of which I was late. Kiyan and I had moved in together by then. My family didn't know about it. I had not given them the correct address to avoid any surprise visits. Kiyan's parents too didn't know about our live-in arrangement. We both knew what our parents were like. More than understanding what Kiyan and I wanted they would have invariably focussed on what society desired of us. We would have been asked to either get engaged first or perhaps married before staying together. I didn't mind a marriage but didn't want to force it on Kiyan either. Living with him, I came to understand that a relationship is inherently private, and before one presents it to society in the garb of marriage, it's better know each other inside out and be certain if it's worthwhile to hold on to the dream of togetherness. Living with Kiyan, I knew we had enough reasons to dream that dream. But he shook me up a little bit when one night I came home and saw him awake, looking perturbed. On other days he used to be asleep by the time I came home, as I was working a night shift while he had a day shift. I inquired if there was a problem. He showed me an email on his laptop. It was his resignation letter. And he had already sent it. My first thought was to ask him what on earth had made him resign all of a sudden when he was heading for a promotion in three months. Then I wondered, whatever may be the reason, why hadn't he discussed it with me? And if he hadn't discussed it with me before sending it, then why was he showing me the email now? I said nothing as all these thoughts were going through my mind.

'I've resigned,' he stated with finality.

'I can see that. Care to explain?' I asked, standing beside him. He shut his laptop and sat on the chair next to it.

'I don't want to work.'

I went blank for a few seconds.

'What do you mean you don't want to work?'

'I mean I don't want to do a regular job any more.'

My inquiring glance egged him on to speak.

'I want to be an author.'

A new, strange kind of silence fell between us. It's hard to describe it. At that moment, the first thing I thought was that our chance of being together was slipping away, or rather, getting postponed. I had made up my mind to inform my parents in a couple of months about us since I was from a typical Baniya family. And I know for a fact that my parents had already started looking for 'prospects' within our community. Girls tend to get married early in our community, and those with jobs even earlier because conservative parents think that working girls become 'bigda hua', after which they can't be married off. The arranged marriage market in our part of the planet is full of deeply insecure people with screwed-up ideas. My thoughts were forced back to the present as Kiyan asked me to respond.

'That's . . . that's nice,' I mumbled. Then I added, 'But you never told me you liked writing. In fact, I used to write as a hobby, but I never knew you too . . .' It was the truth. I used to write a blog. Nothing serious. Just some short stories under a pseudonym.

'I know. But it has been brewing in me for a year now.'

For a year . . . I didn't know whether to give priority to the feeling of hurt that I felt at being kept in the dark or to urge him to continue speaking.

'I thought of telling you many times, but each time I thought if I talked about it, my resolve to follow my heart would weaken.'

We stared at each other for some time, but I couldn't bring myself to say anything. Not knowing what to do with myself, I went

to take a shower. I realized he stood
where he was. I hoped he understood why I
didn't say anything. Whether he wanted to
be something or not was secondary. The fact
that he hadn't made me a part of that plan
was what hurt. I intentionally took a long
shower. I didn't want to face him perhaps.
After almost an hour, I came out. I was
sure he must be waiting for me, but I found
him asleep with a Post-it note on my pillow
that read 'Thanks'. So he had interpreted
my silence as support. Most men suffer from
the bad habit of taking their women for
granted. I didn't sleep well that night.
Kiyan's interpretation was challenging
what I had always thought about us—that we
complemented each other, that we knew each
other the way a blind person understands
Braille. I didn't really sleep the entire
night. When Kiyan woke up in the morning,
I kissed him on the cheek and told him
he could pursue whatever he wanted to and
that I would be there for him, with him,
always and in all ways. I loved him. That
was important. And love, in whichever form,
comes with certain duties. And supporting
him in his decision was my duty.

Kiyan's decision disrupted our life.
But I made sure our standard of living
remained the same. Earlier, we were very

clear about the expenses we incurred—the rent was his, bills were mine. Grocery was mine, weekend food and booze were his. Movies were mine, shopping was his. With Kiyan resigning from the job, we had to take another look at our expenses. The problem was neither of us had worked for long enough to have significant savings. Whatever we earned, we spent. With what he had we could have survived 3-4 months on the existing expense plan, but I asked him to not think about it. I was ready to take care of all expenses. It made us compromise on our weekend plans, but since he had decided to work towards his dream, it was a small sacrifice for the larger goal. Hence, I never complained if I got bored at home during the weekends. I gave up going to movies with friends and shopping sprees.

Whenever I saw Kiyan sitting in a corner of the bedroom beside the window and typing away his debut fiction on his laptop, I felt proud of him. It took guts to give up a settled job and assured prospects, and settle for something uncertain. I did ask him if he had any connection in the publishing world but all he told me was he would think about all that only when he had finished his novel.

My pride held strong for the first three months, after which it was substituted by restlessness. We began to talk less. We made out less. We looked at each other less. Most of the time, he was busy working on his novel or out for research for it. At that point, I didn't know what he was writing about, as Kiyan had requested me not to ask him about it till he finished the story. I could tell he was going through mood swings. Sometimes without any intimation, he would make love to me with such intensity for hours that I thought his deciding to become an author was the best thing that had happened to us. And then there were times when I hugged him, kissed him and all I received were such cold vibes that I wondered if he ever loved me. Our relationship had become dichotomous, and there was no clarity.

When my father said he wanted me to come to Lucknow one weekend because a boy's family from Benaras was coming to 'see' me, I couldn't make any more excuses and was forced to tell him that I was in love with someone. He didn't take it well (as expected), but I guess Ma must have pacified him, since the next time he called (after a week), he said he wanted to meet Kiyan. But the problem was, what could I tell my father? I love this guy who is an ex-engineer who now wants to be an author? Anyone who knows Indian fathers, especially a typical Indian father like mine, would instantly know it's the worst introduction possible. But what option did I have?

7

Some things can only burn, not turn into ashes. My passion for you is one such thing.

The words came rushing to him much like the waves from the calm sea in front of him. Kiyan was standing on the shore in shorts. The light breeze met strong resistance in his muscular body and nearly six-foot frame. The clock had just signalled half past the devil's hour. Except the sea and sand, there was nothing for miles. Right in front of him, though, at some distance, she stood in the sea, water up to her thighs. She had told him they would meet, for the first time, at the dead of the night by the sea. And that's what happened. He had not yet seen her face. And yet he was committed to the image of her in his mind. Looking at her hourglass silhouette in the dark now, he was sure about one thing—Kashti was everything she had made him imagine she was in the last month and a half.

The book launch in Goa had been a different experience altogether since the event had been arranged on a boat and had lasted the duration of a short cruise. It was smooth sailing for the two hours that Kiyan spent with his fans. By now, he was no longer the shy author who felt nervous in front of readers. After six book events on the trot, Kiyan confidently posed with the readers, chit-chatted, signed the books for them and answered all their queries. He thought Kashti would either be at the event or call him right after as he went clubbing alone, but that didn't happen. With Kashti on his mind, he wasn't interested in the looks that a few Russian and Indian women had thrown at him in the club. Kiyan had called it a night and headed back to his hotel. It was only during the wee hours that his phone started ringing, with Kashti's name lighting up on the screen. It was the same number that he had saved in Indore.

'Did I ever tell you,' she asked softly on the phone, pressing the speaker close to her mouth so that her breathing was audible, 'the first thing that came to my mind when I saw you at the Delhi book event?'

'You didn't,' he replied, moistening his dry lips. He could imagine the way the words would manoeuvre her tongue before escaping her mouth.

Kashti then narrated her vivid fantasy of being taken by him on a secluded railway track. By the time she had ended her narration, he felt breathless.

'I'm waiting for you at the beach. Wear just your shorts,' Kashti had said and cut the line.

Kiyan's hotel was a beachside one, and his room had a fantastic view of the sea. Kiyan had drawn his curtains but it had been too dark outside to see anything. He had washed his face and rushed out, not wanting to miss the chance to meet the girl who had slowly become an obsession over the last month.

The darkness around the beach didn't allow Kiyan to conclude if she was wearing anything or not. He was about to wave at her when he noticed her amble towards him. As the waves hit her from behind, he couldn't help but feel the blood between his legs. He wasn't wearing any underwear inside the shorts, as demanded by her, and all he had on his mind as he saw her approach him was where this demand would take them.

'Hi,' she whispered in his ears as her sea-water-drenched body hugged his dry body tight. Wet sand grains clung to him.

'I was waiting for this moment the way a bud waits for spring,' she whispered as she pressed her breasts against his chest, tightening the embrace. He too put his arms around her, realizing she was topless like him. He could feel her hard nipples. As she half broke the embrace, she looked up at him and said, 'Take my name.'

He did.

'I want to taste those lips that had my name on them.'

She slowly sucked his lower lip. He opened his mouth, and she pushed her tongue inside, nudging his. As they smooched, they knelt down together on the wet sand. It took a giant wave to break their smooch, drenching them entirely. She slowly pushed him on the sand, looking deep into his eyes. For the first time, he could see her face—up close and clear. And he couldn't take his eyes off her. Every bit of her was a man's fantasy. She took his hands and pinned them above him as she started kissing his chest. She paused to encircle his nipples with the tip of her tongue and lifted her head up to meet his eyes.

'I know how sensitive you are there,' she said with a naughty smile and sucked his nipples hard. He put his hands on her hair and held them tight as she slipped her mouth further down to his taut abs, tracing along them with her tongue. She grabbed his erect penis over his shorts and started rubbing it.

'That's your instinct or intention?' she asked, holding his erection over his shorts. 'If it's your instinct,' she said, 'then it can happen to anyone. But if it's . . .'

'It's my intention,' he cut her short.

With a sly smile she tugged the shorts down and took them off him. As she placed them on the beach, a small wave came and took them away.

'A wave is like true love. It returns what it takes away with it. The point is whether you are ready to wait for it.'

It was thoughts like these that drew him to her to begin with. He lifted his head slightly and saw her take his penis inside her mouth. All of it. With one hand on her hair, he kept his other hand on the sand and dug his fingers deep in it. As he kept his head back on the sand, involuntarily parting his lips, the pleasure choreographed his expressions. Images of how it had all started flashed in front of him as Kiyan closed his eyes, feeling the cold sand below and the warmth of her mouth between his legs . . . the book event . . . the hotel . . . the photographs . . . the hide and seek . . . the story . . . all of it seemed like a spell to Kiyan. There was something innately fiery in the closeness of their bodies. Every move of hers was arousing him further. He knew nothing about her and yet every second he felt close to something personal within her. The flashes paused as she stopped blowing him. She came up to his face and smooched him. Kashti lifted her back. Kiyan pulled at the knot of her drenched g-string. He threw it away as he felt her vaginal lips on his erection. He was reminded of the fantasy she had told him over the phone. She was now riding him in reality. Except, instead of the railway track, it was the vast sea that was witness to their union. Every time a wave washed the shore, she rode him hard. After some time, when she collapsed against his chest, Kiyan turned her around, holding her tight, and got on top.

His urgency seemed more than hers now. Being on top, he drove towards the climax. His strong thrusts made her moan out loud for the first time. He went on till she felt her voice go hoarse. And then as they locked eyes, he spilled his seed after pulling out.

After they had finished, both lay there, with him on top of her till the first light of dawn broke. Kiyan moved and lay sideways. She caught his hand and stood up. He too stood up. She started ambling towards a series of beach shacks. He was finding it weird to walk naked. To his relief, there was still nobody else on the beach. After taking a few steps, he noticed his drenched shorts on the sand at some distance. The sea had thrown them back. He freed his hand from Kashti's grip and retrieved his briefs. He quickly wore them. By now, the visibility was slightly better. He turned and noticed Kashti was wearing a fresh bikini, which she must have kept earlier by a small stand. He walked towards her, realizing there was a DSLR camera on a tripod next to her.

'This is what brought you to me,' she said, with a twinkle in her eyes as she held the DSLR.

'I remember,' he said, touching the camera. Kashti removed the tripod, slung the camera on her shoulder, and holding Kiyan's hand, led him to one of the shacks on the shore. It was a residential shack.

'I am putting up here,' she said and proceeded to unlock the door of a small house. She pulled Kiyan inside and kicked the door shut behind them. It locked itself.

'Remember I told you I have a gift for you?' she said with a naughty smile and pushed Kiyan onto the single bed in the room.

As Kiyan watched her quietly rummaging through one of her bags, he kept wondering only one thing. Finally, he said it out loud, 'Who are you, Kashti?'

Kashti took out something gift-wrapped from her bag and gave it to Kiyan with a smile.

'This is for you, mister bestselling author.'

Kiyan took it as he heard her say, 'Every one of us has faced a certain storm in our lives, after which nothing remains the way it was. It changes equations, dynamics and old perceptions, and turns known people into strangers.'

'So?' Kiyan asked, unwrapping the gift completely.

'I'm that storm in your life, Kiyan.'

The gift was in his hand now. Kiyan frowned looking at it. He realized something. And he didn't know how to react if what he could see was true. His throat immediately went dry. He felt Kashti's hands on his face. She had cupped it.

'Look at me, mister bestselling author. And look deep,' she said. Her eyes were hypnotic as Kiyan looked into them.

'I shall be straight with you. You'll do as I say, right?'

Kiyan swallowed a lump and found himself nodding.

'You won't upset me ever, right?'

Kiyan nodded again.

'Who do you belong to from now on?'

Kiyan's lips parted with disbelief. If he had had the slightest idea it would lead to this he would have put a stop to it long ago.

'Tell me, who do you belong to from now on?'

'You,' he said, feeling the dryness in his mouth.

'Only me,' she said and planted a kiss on his lips. Kiyan swallowed a lump in his throat and desperately hoped it was all unreal.

'You know, mister bestselling author, your darkness feels like my dawn, my own personal dawn,' Kashti said and smiled at him. And all Kiyan could wonder was how well she had hidden the monster within her with that smile.

* * *

A Girl's Diary

21 March 2016
Monday, 11.15 p.m.

I told Papa all about Kiyan over the phone. I told him I had studied with him during engineering, and that he was working in an MNC like me but was determined to become an author. Papa asked me about the last part twice to make sure he had heard it right. 'Yes, Kiyan wants to become an author,' I repeated. It was his decision. If I had wanted to do something other than be a software engineer, he would have stood by me. I chose to stand by him. I knew Papa would have a problem with it but I had to tell him clearly lest he kept looking for grooms for me. In fact, since his elder brother (my Bade Papa) had arranged white-collar husbands for his two daughters, my Papa too wanted a white-collar guy for me. Being his only daughter, all the focus was on me. And thus my choice, I knew, would invariably be taken as defiance. The result was what I had expected. Papa stopped talking to me. That year was my first Diwali that I did not celebrate with family. It's so strange that the same set of people who have helped you grow into a fine adult are ready to break off all ties over the biggest decision of your life. But it was my decision to be with Kiyan. Day in and day out I saw him work on his stories, and I kept telling myself I had made the right decision. I believed that one day my family would understand their short-sightedness. However, it wasn't like a vendetta against them.

Thinking back, I feel happy about my decision. But trust me, it wasn't easy. On his path to becoming a bestselling author, the responsibility somehow fell on me to 'mother' him. Taking care of all types of shit is the foremost priority of such a responsibility. To his readers, Kiyan seems like a guy who would be a dream boyfriend, but that's not true.

Dating an author is not the best thing in the world. Trust me on this. For that matter, nor is dating any creative person. For starters, they get bored easily. They get restless easily. And the ones they are closest to are the easiest target for all their emotional tantrums. And worst of all, they mentally inhabit a different world half the time. I took time to understand this after I noticed distinct behavioural changes in Kiyan while he was working on his manuscript. He started having mood swings. Mainly because sitting at home all day was so new for him. The same liberal-minded Kiyan whom I had adored and who used to give me space (of course, after the college break-up) suddenly reverted to his former possessive self. He never used to comment on my dressing style earlier, but one day when I was supposed to go to a college reunion of sorts with a few batchmates, Kiyan asked me not to wear torn jeans. If there had been any sensible reason for it, and he hadn't said it in a dominating manner, I would have considered his request. I can take everything, but I can't take someone bossing over me. Whoever it may be. The fact that he said I shouldn't wear them made me adamant about wearing the jeans. And I did. We had a bad fight. A violent one rather. This was also the beginning of a new trait I noticed in Kiyan that day. Whenever he was angry at me, he would break something or the other. As if he needed an outlet to vent the violent energy. It was scary. I went to the reunion wearing what I wanted to, but when I came back he refused to open the door. There are times when you apologize, and there are times when you take a stand. A smart girl knows when to do what. I called my colleague and went to stay with her. I was there for a week until Kiyan came and apologized to me. I realized it is important to make your partner realize your worth. Too much of ego massaging and submissiveness gets you taken for granted on an everyday basis, and that's the worst disease that can take over a relationship. Your partner should always have the fear of losing you. That fear keeps love young forever. If he doesn't feel it, it is your duty to implant it in him.

After I returned to the flat, Kiyan was on his best behaviour for a long time until another weird tendency of his started bothering me. Earlier, whenever we had sex, he would wear protection, but suddenly he started demanding unprotected sex. I didn't know the reason for it. Kiyan only told me he didn't enjoy it with protection. This, after we had been doing it for almost a year? And the more he immersed himself into the manuscript, into his story, the more he lost sight of the fact that I wasn't a sex toy that he could simply use any which way he wanted. If I demanded protection, he didn't touch me for a month. I gave in to his demands when I thought it was safe, but I couldn't risk it otherwise because he never pulled out on time. It frustrated me, and I'm sure it frustrated him as well, but I couldn't understand this dumping of desire on one's partner. Why does this happen in a relationship? So many times, we do things because we are with someone and not because our heart is in it. Of course, we convince ourselves we do so out of love towards the person, but is it really that? Can anything that happens due to some kind of pressure be love? Pressure means force and force seems to me the antithesis of love. Love is natural, it just happens, then blossoms and then proliferates, but can never be forced, never be generated out of pressure. Then what was it that Kiyan was trying to do by thrusting his demands on me? So often I wanted to get inside his head and see what was going on in there. Till then, I had never asked him about his story or characters. I too used to write—bits and pieces of poems, short stories, nothing major. Nothing serious. But I did understand a creative mind. It is unpredictable. Untameable. And certainly incorrigible. People shall forever worship the hero they see, but I feel the real heroes behind a creative mind are always the people who put up with the person's crazy idiosyncrasies. Probably it was this realization that stopped me every time I thought of giving up on Kiyan. It's not him; it's the way he is. There's a difference. And only people in love can spot the difference.

Today, finally, all your book travels have ended, Kiyan. I was so waiting for this day. And I know so have you. I'll end my rant here. I don't know how much of this diary will make sense to you, Kiyan, but I wanted you to know all the hurt and pain I have been on the receiving end of in the years we have been together. Don't think all these were complaints. It was just my way of sharing them with you. I believe if two people decide to spend a life together, they should at least be open about their hurt to the other, otherwise there is no point claiming they are in love. Next week onwards, a new chapter will begin for us, and I just wanted to be as ready as you are. I shall gift this diary to you soon. But whenever you read it, don't tell me you have. Just come up to me and hug me tightly. Pick me up and make rough love to me the way you always do. Yeah, for once, I may just enjoy it. Haha.

In every which way, yours,
Anaysha

* * *

8

Anaysha was both happy and anxious. Happy because it was the day when a near-impossible dream of hers was about to come true. She was supposed to get engaged to the man she loved, the one she had fought for, the one she had stood by through thick and thin and the one who meant the world to her—Kiyan Roy. Not many people are lucky enough to get a chance to live with the one they want to live with and have the other person feel the same way. Anaysha was ecstatic to know she was one of those people. The other, of course, was Kiyan. His book tour had ended the other day in Goa. Anaysha had been counting the days since the book tour had begun. She had gift-wrapped the diary in which she was penning their love story with absolute honesty. Anaysha wanted to gift it to Kiyan right after they exchanged rings later in the evening. It wasn't just a diary. It was a love story with glimpses of thoughts that she had never shared with Kiyan. And she wanted him to know it all when they got married. She wanted him to marry someone who was transparent about whatever she had ever thought of him at each point in their love story. The realization would help further solidify their relationship post-marriage.

Anaysha had introduced Kiyan to her family for the first time in person when he had made it to the headlines in *Lucknow Times* of *Times of India*. She knew it would end all the apprehension in her family. And it did. Her father was suddenly proud of her choice, and her cousins were all ga-ga about the fact that the Gupta family of Chowk, Lucknow, would have a celebrity bridegroom. The Gupta family met the Roy family for dinner in BBQ and decided on the engagement and marriage dates. The marriage was fixed for six months after the engagement.

Anaysha's parents and a couple of cousins came to Delhi to shop for her engagement. She bought an emerald-studded green lehenga choli for herself, booked the best make-up person in Lucknow and asked one of her college friends who had become a professional photographer to capture the engagement in all its vibrancy.

Kiyan had called in the morning. Anaysha found it odd that he was still in Goa. He told her everything was going according to plan as his publisher had arranged some seminars and college visits in Goa, and that he would land in Lucknow in the afternoon and be at the banquet hall on time.

The evening began with her cousins mischievously taking away Anaysha's phone and refusing to give it back. They said they would not let her be in touch with Kiyan till the rings were exchanged. They joked that if he called, they would talk to him instead of her, and made plans to say all sorts of silly things to him. The engagement was to happen at 8 p.m., but till 7 p.m. there was no sign of the Roy family. Anaysha's father called Mr Roy, who told him to talk to Kiyan. Anaysha's father called Kiyan, but he didn't pick up.

'If there is any problem then we should sit and talk it out,' Anaysha's father told her. The atmosphere at the banquet hall was one of tension and frenzy.

Anaysha, all dressed up for the occasion, herself called up Kiyan thrice, but none of her calls were taken. It was 9 p.m. Everyone was in the banquet hall with no clue about what was going on. Mr Gupta, who had personally gone to Kiyan's place in Lucknow, came back looking harassed and said, 'Kiyan has asked his family not to attend the engagement. I tried my best, but they refused to tell me anything further.' Anaysha had seen her father tensed before, mainly about his garment business, but this was different. This was a matter of pride.

Suddenly, Anaysha's phone rang. One of the cousins saw Kiyan's name on the screen and shouted out, 'Jiju ka phone hai.' The cousin gave the phone to Anaysha.

The entire Gupta family was looking at her and hoping whatever the issue was, it got sorted soon.

'Hello?' Anaysha said with a dry mouth. She had an inkling it wasn't anything good she would hear. 'Where are you, Kiyan? We are all waiting for you. Even your parents are acting weird,' she said.

'Anaysha, I'm sorry, we have to call off the engagement.'

'What do you mean? What happened? Where are you?'

'I'm in Goa. I didn't know how to tell you this. I didn't want to tell you this today especially, but . . .'

'What is it Kiyan?'

'I stopped loving you long ago. I don't think we should be together.'

Anaysha's phone fell from her hand. People rushed to catch her before she collapsed to the ground.

Part 2: Snatch

Part 2: Snatch

9

'I don't believe this,' Kashti hugged Kiyan tightly and gave him a hard peck after he broke up with Anaysha over the phone. Kiyan kept still. A few seconds later, he too put his hands around her back and pressed her close. *He had to.* From now on, he would have to do a lot more than what he had just been forced to say to Anaysha on the phone. Kiyan was intelligent enough to realize that.

When Kiyan arrived in Goa a day before the book event, he had been booked at The Lalit for the night, but of course he had checked out and come to the shack where Kashti was putting up, and on her insistence, shifted there with her after she had given him the gift. Though he had told Kashti about his impending engagement to Anaysha, he knew Kashti was in no mood to listen to anything.

'You never told me about Anaysha before,' she'd said.

'There was no need to.' Kiyan tried hard but couldn't suppress his haplessness.

'You were committed and yet you were pursuing me. You were committed and yet you didn't stop me at the gym or by the beach? What does that say about your relationship, Kiyan?'

Kiyan was quiet.

'That you wanted to be snatched by me. I did what you desired,' Kashti said and kissed his lips. A few seconds later, she added, 'I don't believe this. THE Kiyan Roy is my boyfriend now. Wow!' Kashti broke the embrace and looked deep into his eyes. She commanded, 'Tell me it's true.' Kiyan took a few seconds before saying, 'It's true.'

'Tell me it's true.'

'It's true.'

'Tell me it's true, Kiyan.'

'It's true, Kashti.'

She planted a hard kiss on his lips, sucking at his lower lip and releasing it with a naughty smirk.

'You don't know how long I have waited for this. This is like an impossible dream come true.' Kashti let go of Kiyan and climbed onto her bed.

'Should I shout like Tarzan?'

A tight smile escaped Kiyan.

'What about Anaysha?'

Kashti's smile dried up.

'I'll let you know. There's time for it.'

'There's no time. I'll have to inform Anaysha.'

Kashti got off the bed and came dangerously close to Kiyan, whispering almost threateningly, 'Do you think it will make a difference if she knows it today or on the day of the engagement?'

Kiyan didn't know what to say while Kashti smirked and said, 'Let's not bring her between us any more. She is history, right?'

Kiyan only stared at her.

'Right?' Kashti repeated. Kiyan nodded. The gift she had given him was her way of binding him to her. The way an owner puts a collar on a pet.

A sudden smile appeared on Kashti's face as she said, 'Then let's enjoy our stay in Goa.' She took a couple of steps backwards, still on the bed, and raised her hand to take off her bikini top. Walking with the gait of a cat, she climbed off the bed and turned around before entering the bathroom. 'I know you don't know much about me, mister bestselling author, but how about we start with this—I don't like to shower alone,' she said and entered the bathroom. Kiyan glanced helplessly at the unwrapped gift lying on the table beside him and with his jaw set tight, entered the bathroom. He knew he had been trapped.

In the 10 days that followed, Kiyan realized Kashti had planned each moment of their stay beforehand. Where to breakfast, where to eat lunch, where to dine, where to club, where to make love, all of it as if she knew he was going to say yes to her, as if her following him across book events was part of a hunting process. And the hunt had been successful. He was indeed that easy a prey. Once, she made him park their rented bike in the open for a quickie. They stopped under the sultry sun of Goa when everyone else was taking a siesta. Their tanned bodies shone as they made out on the bike parked by the beach. In the evening, they watched the sunset together, sipping freshly brewed local beer. Though Kiyan was physically with her, every second he was dreading the moment when he would have to tell Anaysha. Every time she called in those 10 days, he lied to her, saying he had had to stay back in Goa due to some college visits and seminars that his publisher had organised. The problem was he couldn't even come clean if he wanted to. He would have to lie to her. But it wasn't a complete lie either. How do you tell your girlfriend when she is about to become your fiancée that you are done with her, especially when you don't totally believe it yourself?

On what was supposed to have been D-day, Kiyan and Kashti were cuddling in bed after two hours of marathon sex. Kiyan's phone rang for the umpteenth time since the afternoon. He had kept it on silent after messaging his parents that he wouldn't be in Lucknow and wasn't interested in getting engaged any more. No more explanations. Though he had been in touch with Anaysha till this morning, with her still believing they were going to get engaged tonight, he hadn't messaged her since then. It was Anaysha who called him as he lay in bed cuddling. He stared at his phone till it became a missed call. Anaysha called again, but he didn't pick up. When it happened the third time, Kiyan heard Kashti say, 'Why don't you take the call?' Kiyan was quiet.

'You asked me what to do about her a few days ago. Well, this is the right time. Tell her the new truth about your life.'

'But . . .'

'Just pick up the damn phone and call her. Tell her you don't love her any more.'

The ease with which Kashti said it made him wish he could be that cold with Anaysha.

'Do it if you really love me, Kiyan,' she said.

Kiyan sat up. He swallowed a lump and saw Kashti dial Anaysha for him. She pressed the speaker button, and together they heard the phone ring. It was picked up on the second ring.

'Where are you, Kiyan? We are all waiting for you. Even your parents are acting weird.'

Kiyan's mind went blank. He didn't register anything except that he told Anaysha that he had fallen out of love with her. And the moment he said it Kashti ended the call, hugging him tightly.

'You just proved to me that you really love me, Kiyan,' she said, breaking the hug.

What had he just proved to Anaysha? Kiyan thought.

* * *

Anaysha's Diary

I never thought this diary of mine would see more ink. I never thought I would be the one who would tear open the gift-wrap of this diary. I never thought you would do this to me, Kiyan. *This!*

It's been a week since he humiliated me in front of my family. 'I stopped loving you long ago.' I will never forget those words of his. They have been imprinted on my mind like audio gets recorded on a tape. They can't be erased. They won't be taken back. They won't ever perish.

I remember how my family was behaving when I came to my senses that night. Instead of being empathetic, every elder felt it was their duty to accuse me. As if I was at fault for the family's embarrassment. As if I had asked Kiyan not to attend our engagement and humiliate my family and myself. Nobody told me, 'Don't worry, everything will be all right.' Instead, everyone ignored me. Apart from my cousins who were children and too young to fully understand the situation, nobody talked to me. Why? Because I chose Kiyan. I had gone against everyone to be the first girl in the entire family to get engaged to someone who didn't belong to my community, and most importantly, to someone who I had picked myself. Never before had a Gupta girl gone ahead and married someone of her choice. And I know that after what happened last week, no other girl will. Or will be allowed to. Till last week I was a rebel for my cousins. Now, they think of the same person as an example of what can happen if you don't listen to elders and dare to take your decisions on your own. I have never felt so helpless, so defeated or so unwanted ever before. Not all of these feelings together at least. So many times I wanted to call Kiyan back, message him and ask him what suddenly went wrong. What did I do? I fucking invested 5 years in him, supported him, stood by him and tolerated all his shitty behaviour, only because I loved him. And what did I get? Not only was I ditched and had my heart broken, but I also became an excuse for my family to label me as an immature ass.

I haven't dared to look at myself in the mirror since that day. But I can feel my eyes have swollen. I haven't had a proper bath, and my head feels heavy and reels at times. The family doctor came to check on me and said my blood pressure has increased. I keep myself locked in my room with no connection to the outside world. Once in a while I access WhatsApp and check Kiyan's DP. Not to ask him anything but to ask myself what I saw in him that didn't let me see the real him? What was it that blinded me so much and for so long? The only good thing about the public humiliation is that no one from my community will now send a proposal for me. At least not for a year. I overheard Papa and Mumma talking about it.

While writing in this diary, I realized I couldn't stay here any more. There is negativity in my own house. I think that's the crux of irony for an Indian girl. Of all the places in the world, her own house at times becomes the worst kind of hell for her. There are so many thoughts in my mind right now that I don't know which one to focus on. On the nights that followed the engagement fiasco, I kept wondering why Kiyan would say what he did on the day of the engagement? Why couldn't he tell me before? Not that it would have changed much, except, maybe I would have been spared this kind of public humiliation. Did he want that for me? In all these years, was he brewing hatred for me that

I mistook for love? But why would he? I haven't done anything evil to him. I shy away from taking credit, but the fact will always remain that he is THE Kiyan Roy today because I stood by him when even his parents had washed their hands off him. It was my hard-earned money that fuelled his dreams. Then what did he mean by saying he had fallen out of love with me? Out of love, is that even possible? Unless, of course, it wasn't love to begin with, but we convinced ourselves it was. Every day we give our minds so much bullshit to feed on that in turn it gives us enough illusions as fodder.

I don't know if we will ever meet, Kiyan, but if we do I just want to ask you one simple fucking question:

WHY?

WHY!

10

Kiyan and Kashti stayed in Goa for a week more after he cancelled the engagement. During this time, they cancelled and rebooked their air tickets twice. For Kiyan, saying no to Anaysha had been a lesson in self-realization. It was something he had never thought he would be able to do. But he had done it. A week had passed by without any contact with Anaysha. How easily he had slipped out of a long relationship and got into another as if it were slippers he was changing. Even if the breakup hadn't happened by choice, the decision of choosing Kashti over Anaysha had been his.

What amazed Kiyan was that Kashti too was living in Gurgaon, just like Anaysha and he were till he visited Goa. When they booked a cab from Delhi airport, Kashti made it clear they were going to live together from now on. He was told he could bring his stuff as she had already made space in her flat. His amazement went up a notch when Kashti directed the cab driver to the same apartment where Anaysha and he used to live together. Every time he had flown back from the book events, it was this apartment he had returned to. But why was Kashti taking him there? It was evident she had done her research, but did she want him to collect his stuff first? Would he find Anaysha there?

'This is where I live,' he said.

All he got in response was a mysterious smile. They stepped out of the lift on the same floor where Kiyan and Anaysha lived. When he went right, towards his flat, Kashti turned left.

'From now on, you will be living here, Kiyan, not there,' she said, pulling him towards her.

'You were our neighbour?' Kiyan wanted to but couldn't hide the surprise in his voice.

'For the last six months. Anaysha and I have seen each other many times but have never spoken.'

'But why?'

'I don't know why we didn't talk,' Kashti said and unlocked the door to her flat. By then, Kiyan had noticed his flat was locked, which meant Anaysha wasn't there. He quickly went towards Kashti's flat and stepped in.

'I mean, why were you living here as our neighbour?'

'I wanted to steal you from Anaysha,' Kashti said in a naughty tone and moved forward to draw the curtains of the drawing room. The sun rays seemed to kiss her as she stood by the window. She turned around and said, 'I'm kidding. It was just a coincidence.'

Something told Kiyan not to believe her. His eyes fell on his trilogy on a shelf. He frowned and then asked,

'I know I asked you this before, but I will ask you again. Did you read my books?'

'You mean, was I your fan?'

Kiyan nodded.

'Nope,' she said. 'I bought the books after I saw you at the New Delhi book launch.'

'If you didn't know me or my work, why did you attend the launch?'

'I didn't. One of my friends did. And I came there to click her picture with you. And see where we are today. She is yet to know I have fucked her dream author ten times by now. And each time he has given me a belly-contracting, toe-curling orgasm,' Kashti said, coming over to Kiyan and placing her hands around his neck. He gave her an unsure smile.

'So, how do you like your new pad, mister bestselling author?'

Mister bestselling author—she had used this to address him after a long time now. He looked around. The flooring was wood. There was an LED television on the wall, below which was a long cabinet that had three handmade dolls on each side. On the opposite side was a rack on which there were coloured bottles. Above these, on the wall, were framed photos of Kiyan's close-ups, the ones that Kashti had clicked during the first book event in New Delhi.

'See, you were here with me even when you weren't,' she said, making herself comfortable on a two-seater recliner by the window in the room. Kiyan smiled at her casually and said, 'This is pretty cosy.'

'Thank you. I'm honoured you like it. The one you shared with Anaysha was pretty dull. I don't like anything dull.'

Without reacting to what she had said, Kiyan went to the window, which had a handmade wind chime with the alphabet K hanging from each of the tubes.

'They say if you fantasize hard about what you desire, it is given to you,' Kashti said, looking at Kiyan. He held on to the wind chimes and looked at her.

'I've been fantasizing about you every night since I saw you, Kiyan. Nothing mattered to me except you.'

'Did you see me for the first time at the launch?'

'Yes. At New Delhi.'

That's like 9 weeks ago. In 9 weeks, she snatched me away from Anaysha, a person I had a relationship with for 5 years, Kiyan wondered. What did that say about Kashti, and more importantly, about him? Did he move away from Anaysha because it was always supposed to be so, and Kashti was only a means to an end? Wasn't Kashti's 'gift' the major reason this had happened? Or was he awaiting an opportunity like this to move out of Anaysha's life and the 'gift' had only helped his subconscious cause?

Kiyan tapped his shirt pocket and then jeans pocket, and remembered he hadn't been allowed to bring his cigarettes on the flight.

'I'll be back in two minutes. Need to buy some cigarettes,' Kiyan said, opening the main door.

'Okay. Let me prepare some lunch for us. I'm so hungry. Would pasta with white sauce do?'

'Certainly,' he said and locked the door behind him.

Kiyan went out and called for the elevator, all the while staring at the door of the flat where he used to live with Anaysha. It was still locked. He wished he never had to face her again. What would he even tell her? The truth about the 'gift'? If he did that, then the remaining respect that Anaysha may have for him—just may—would vanish instantly. In a few days, he would have to convince Kashti to move out from here.

The elevator doors opened. He stepped in and pressed the ground-floor button. His mind was focussed on Anaysha for the first time since he had decided to call off the engagement. Was he the same person who had helped her in the ATM in Wakhnaghat long ago and fallen in love with her? What happened to that love? What happened to that person? What happened to that promise he had made to himself back then that if she became his partner he would have nothing else to ask for in life? With new realizations, the old promises fade. With new desires, the old self transforms. With new emotional pursuits, the old miles lose significance.

The elevator reached the ground floor. The doors opened. Kiyan was about to step out when he froze, seeing Anaysha standing there. One of the security guards was helping her with her bags. He entered the elevator. Kiyan took a few steps backwards. Anaysha stepped in. Their eyes remain locked. Neither of them blinked. She looked beaten by life; he looked cornered by it.

'Tenth floor, madam?' the guard asked.

Anaysha nodded. The guard pressed the button and turned to ask Kiyan, 'Tenth floor, sir?' Kiyan nodded. The guard didn't know why the two weren't talking since he thought Kiyan and Anaysha were now husband and wife.

Anaysha could feel her anger bubbling. She controlled her impulse to hit him. She wanted to talk to him and yet wanted him to initiate it. After all, it was he who had called off the engagement. Kiyan was too tongue-tied to utter anything. This was what he had been afraid of when he had realized Kashti lived in the same building as them. He had planned to quickly move his stuff out of the flat before there was a chance of running into Anaysha. But now there was no option. And this, he knew, would prove to be more hurtful than anything he had felt before.

The elevator stopped at the tenth floor. The guard was the first one to step out with Anaysha's luggage. Neither Kiyan nor Anaysha moved.

'Hey, didn't you go yet?' Kashti asked, standing by the elevator door.

* * *

Anaysha's Diary

How does one get over the minute details of a relationship? Ultimately these are the details that magnify themselves and keep tormenting us. You keep thinking how you wasted your time and thought you were being smart. And you have nothing to say because your own judgement of the person outsmarted you. It not only weakens you emotionally but also tells you how incapable you may be of understanding the one you claim you love. I think that's the worst thing possible—not understanding the person you claim you love even though you have spent so much time with them. It makes you feel wrong about your own self. And then there is the moment-of-truth question whose answer alters the way you perceive love. If you couldn't understand the person by staying with them for so long, how will you ever understand someone? And if you can't understand someone, how are you going to love them? And if not love, then why else would you want to settle down with someone?

These thoughts tormented me so much that I finally decided I would rather get

back to Gurgaon than stay in Lucknow. The
faces of my family members had become a
kaleidoscope, wherein I could see that
ill-fated evening reflected again and
again. I was a prisoner of my thoughts.
That's why I took the decision to pack
and leave home. Papa tried to strike a
deal with me. He said he would let me
work for one more year and live the way I
wanted to, but after that I would have to
listen to him. By the last part he meant
I would have to get married and leave my
job, since most guys from our community
were settled in Lucknow or nearby, working
in their family businesses. I didn't say
anything. He understood I agreed. One
year is a long time. After Kiyan left
me humiliated, every moment seemed longer
than it actually was. I was used to calling
him from office every day. I didn't know
what to do when I couldn't call him. I
told myself a thousand times that he is a
dog and a coward who left me, but I still
couldn't help the urge to call him. I'm so
used to telling him 'have your coffee', 'do
take a noon nap', 'don't overwork yourself
in the gym', 'don't forget to have your
protein shake' that I felt my day was
incomplete without uttering these things.
It was a pathetic, pathetic feeling. I

know I'm acting like a loser but I still can't get over it. Adding 'used to' to all the things Kiyan and I did together is terrible. I wonder if Kiyan too feels the same way. I would never know. But what I really want to know is what made him reject me. Or if it's a 'who'.

11

'You came back so quickly?' Kashti asked, looking straight at Kiyan. She knew who was standing beside him. She was avoiding looking directly at the woman she had stolen Kiyan from.

'I'm yet to go,' Kiyan said.

'I thought you had already gone, Kiyan,' Anaysha said curtly.

The guard kept the luggage by Anaysha's doorstep and stepped into the elevator. The elevator door shut after Kiyan and Anaysha got off.

Anaysha kept looking at Kashti. She now conclusively knew the 'what' was a 'who'. This girl standing in front of her had made Kiyan forget whatever she had done for him in all these years.

'I think we can do with a little introduction. What say, Kiyan?' Kashti said to him and then directed her gaze towards Anaysha, saying, 'Hi, I'm Kashti, Kiyan's girlfriend.' She extended her hand. Anaysha shook it, and said, 'I'm Anaysha. Kiyan's . . .' She almost choked but realized it wouldn't be good to cry in front of these people who didn't give a damn about her tears.

'I'm Kiyan's college friend,' Anaysha managed to say. Like a movie, her relationship with Kiyan played in her mind—from the ATM in Wakhnaghat and the night train from Chandigarh to the house party in Lucknow to their life together in Gurgaon. Had it really happened? And the guy she had loved so genuinely had the audacity to bring the girl who had snatched him away from her to their place.

'You two are living here?' Anaysha asked. Kiyan was about to respond but Kashti spoke up instead, 'Yes, here,' and gestured towards her flat. Anaysha wanted to know if it was Kiyan's decision to be her neighbour. He never had such a nasty sense of humour.

'Nice to meet you, Anaysha,' Kashti said with a hint of condescension. 'Excuse us please. I'm in the middle of preparing our lunch, and Kiyan needs to get some cigarettes for himself.'

Our. The word spliced open Anaysha's heart. She looked at Kiyan once, her jaw locked tightly with the effort of this interaction, mumbled a soft 'okay', turned and unlocked her door. Kiyan saw her go in and lock the door behind her.

'Are you going?' Kashti asked.

Kiyan nodded and pressed the elevator button. He wanted to escape quickly and pretend the encounter hadn't happened.

When he returned after smoking half a pack of cigarettes, he found Kashti waiting for him, with lunch ready. He joined her at the table. As he speared some fusilli in white sauce on his fork, Kiyan asked, 'Where are you from, Kashti?'

'Huh?'

The question took her by surprise, though Kiyan didn't understand why. It was an obvious question. In fact, the surprising part was that Kiyan was asking such a basic thing about her only after moving in with her.

'I'm from Kanpur.'

Kiyan heard her response, but his mind was still on the fact that he had dumped his long-term girlfriend. *Rather, he was made to.* The last part, he knew, didn't matter any more. He only wished the 'gift' Kashti had given him in Goa could be done away with like a bad plot point in a novel. But it was real. And thus all the more scary. A girl who could gift him such a thing could do anything. The 'gift' silently screamed the message 'Don't mess with me, Kiyan, otherwise . . .'

'Does your family live there?' he asked.

Kashti paused, sipped a little water, and with an amused face said, 'Someone is interviewing me.'

'What to do?' He met her eyes and continued, 'Not everyone can go around following people for information.'

'How I wish you had done that. Anyway, Mom and Dad live in the US, with my elder sister. They come to visit twice a year.'

'And they are okay with their daughter living alone in Delhi?'

'I'm not alone. My uncle lives in Pitampura. But I don't like to live with him and his family. More so now that I have you.'

Kiyan nodded while swallowing a tiny bite.

'I would love to meet your family though,' Kashti said, scooping up a little more pasta from the bowl and putting it on her plate.

'Sure. They are in Lucknow.'

'Even Anaysha is from Lucknow, right?'

Hearing Anaysha's name from Kashti's mouth made him uncomfortable. He nodded.

'How long were you guys in a relationship?'

'Five years.' Kiyan felt his throat dry up when he said it. He looked up to notice Kashti was giggling.

'What?' he asked.

'5 years. And I snatched you from her in 9 weeks. Wow! I so love myself.' This time her giggle had an evil ring to it. It wasn't the giggle he had heard on the phone before, which had aroused him. It was the kind that reminded him that only such a girl could have gifted him what she did.

Kiyan's phone, kept on the sofa, rang. He excused himself and went to pick it up. Natasha, his editor, was calling him.

'Hey Natasha, how are you?'

'I'm good. How are you?'

'Good here.'

'Kiyan, why didn't you tell me before? I could have asked the marketing team to make it even bigger than what it is now.'

'Tell you what? I didn't get it.'

'That you have made your official profile on Facebook, Instagram and Twitter for the first time. That's something big, Kiyan, and we should have cashed in on it in a bigger way. I know you made TOI feature it in Delhi Times, but you should have informed us first.'

Kiyan went quiet. Then he glanced at Kashti. She was eating her fusilli so peacefully and with such attention that he was almost convinced she had nothing to do with anything.

'I'll call you back, Natasha,' Kiyan said, his jaw taut.

12

'It was you, right?' Kiyan demanded, standing where he was.

'As in?' Kashti lifted her head up.

'As in you have made profiles on all major social media in my name.'

'Oh yes. I did,' Kashti said in a matter-of-fact manner.

'And the TOI thing?'

'A friend's elder brother works there.'

'But why did you do it?' Kiyan asked, moving towards her a tad aggressively.

'You need it baby,' Kashti said, unaffected. She stood up, done with her lunch, and picked up both their plates. 'How much longer will you remain a recluse?'

'And you did that without my permission,' he said and watched Kashti casually amble to the kitchen and appear seconds later as if his words didn't mean much to her. It fuelled his anger.

'I don't want you to do anything without my permission any more,' he said firmly.

All he heard as a response was a loud thud. Kashti had locked the bedroom door behind her. Kiyan called up Natasha.

'Sorry, I couldn't inform you guys as one of my friends arranged the social media thing for me. But I promise I shall keep you guys in the loop with whatever I do in the future.'

'That's fine, Kiyan. Actually, you did the right thing. We were thinking of telling you that by being a recluse, you won't get as many readers as you will if you start interacting with them personally via social media. Readers always like to connect with the author who gave them sleepless nights for all the right reasons, if you know what I mean.'

'Yeah, I do,' Kiyan replied and heard the bedroom door unlock. Kashti came out and then walked straight out of the main door without saying anything or even looking at Kiyan. The main door locked behind her with an even louder thud than the bedroom door had half a minute ago.

'We are already in talks with a few social content creators who will promote this news. The marketing team told me that they did a survey and learnt you have a tremendous female fan following. So, they are trying to build you up as Mr Desirable from the next book onwards.'

'Thank you so much, Natasha.'

'This is just the beginning, Kiyan. Just work hard on the next manuscript and leave the rest to us.'

'Sure, I will.'

The moment Kiyan cut the phone, he called Kashti. The phone was switched off. Kiyan wondered what he should do, and in the end, opted to wait for her to come back. With Kashti gone, he thought, it was a good idea to check the flat out. To his surprise, except for the refrigerator, every wardrobe, every drawer, the television cabinet and the bar cabinet were locked. Kiyan found it suspicious, but there was nothing he could do until Kashti was back. There was a small bookshelf above the study table in the bedroom. The table had academic books on it, but the shelf only had fiction. There were broadly two categories—romance and thrillers. Kiyan picked up one of the books and lay on the bed, reading it. Since the encounter with Anaysha, he couldn't help but feel guilty. Had it not been for the 'gift' Kashti had given him, he wouldn't have ditched Anaysha this way. He wouldn't have broken up with her at all. Prior to the 'gift', he was attracted to Kashti. He still was. But he would have gone ahead with his engagement. He would have not told Anaysha anything about what happened during the book events and gone on to marry her. If Kashti had continued pursuing him . . . Kiyan couldn't think further. Of what he understood of Kashti, in the last week in Goa he had realized there was one major difference between the two women. Kashti was about possession while Anaysha was about freedom.

'I'm sorry, Anaysha,' he muttered to himself, closing his eyes as he put down the book. The exhaustion of Goa caught up with him as he shut his eyes. He fell asleep thinking of Anaysha's face when he had seen her outside the elevator.

When he opened his eyes, he felt some weight on his pelvis. He tried but couldn't move his hands. He opened his eyes completely to see Kashti sitting atop him, giggling. He had no idea when she came in.

'You look so edible when you're asleep, mister bestselling author.'

'What's this, Kashti?' Kiyan said, trying to sit up, but in vain. His hands were tied together with a soft, furry handcuff.

'Kashti69Kiyan,' she said, with amusement on her face.

'What?'

'KashtiheartKiyan.'

'What are you saying? And unlock me. Now!' Kiyan raised his voice.

'The first one is the username, and the second one is the password to all your social media accounts.'

'I'll take charge of those accounts the moment you unlock me. Now, come on.'

'Please do so. But while your hands are cuffed, I'm in charge,' she said and took her top off. She looked straight at him and unhooked her bra. Kiyan couldn't help but notice her nipples were erect. The sight of those firm 32D breasts made his nut sack tighten, but he said. 'I'm not in the mood right now, Kashti. Just release me.'

She kept looking at him for some time. He remained still. She reached for his shorts and pulled them down along with his underwear. Looking at his semi erection, she said, 'Well, I disagree, mister bestselling author.' She placed her fingers on his balls and started caressing them gently.

'Goddamnit,' Kiyan said in a muffled voice.

In no time, he had a hard-on.

'Someone is more obedient than you,' Kashti said with a mischievous smile.

'Let's do it later tonight. Not now . . .' Kiyan stopped midway because by then Kashti had put a condom on his penis. She tugged her shorts down and asked, 'Were you saying something?'

'Put it in, will you?' Kiyan couldn't take the ache any more. Kashti wasn't Anaysha; he had concluded correctly. Kashti had her way. With Anaysha, he had his.

'That's why I love you, Kiyan. You give in to me,' she said and slowly took in his entire length. Kiyan closed his eyes as pleasure blanketed him. He couldn't see Kashti grab his phone from near his pillow and call Anaysha while riding him. She pressed the mute button and put the call on speaker. When she saw that the call had been picked up she kept it back beside the pillow and started moaning like a kitten, saying Kiyan's name out loud, with an evil smile on her face. She bent down and bit him hard on his chest. Kiyan grunted out Kashti's name. One glance at the phone told Kashti the call was still on. As the seconds ticked by on the timer, Kashti felt a strong orgasm build up inside her.

This was only the beginning.

* * *

Anaysha's Diary

First staying with the girl on the same floor as ours and now this phone call? What does Kiyan want to prove by calling me while having sex with somebody else? Did he think I wouldn't be able to take it? When did he become such a sadist? What did I do to him to deserve this? When the girl moaned his name on the phone I only felt injured, but every time I heard him say her name, something burned in me. It was like whatever was in my head turned real. Since the time I saw the two outside the elevator, I couldn't stop myself thinking about what they may be doing. I was in the

drawing room when I heard the flat door
close. I did look through the peephole and
saw Kashti leaving. I somehow resisted
the urge to go to Kiyan and ask him why he
had come up with me in the elevator when
he was actually going down. Did he have
anything to tell me? And why was he quiet
when we reached our floor? Was it because
of Kashti? Was he hiding something from
her too like he was hiding information
from me about Kashti?

I've come to realize that to pull
oneself out of a relationship, away from
thoughts about a person, from the habits
that develop while being in a relationship
and from the person you become by being
with another person, is the most difficult
thing to do. And it requires time. Since
the time I took that vulgar phone call
last night, I felt a vehement urge to get
back at Kiyan. I don't have many friends
here. All I had was Kiyan. And he was the
world to me until the world decided to
leave me.

This evening, I donned light make-up
after a long time and went to a disc—
Striker. I had heard from my colleagues
that it was a good place. My plan was
clear. I would pick some random guy, bring
him to my flat and have sex with him.

Only sex. No emotions, no love, nothing. I wanted to somehow dwarf the humiliation that Kiyan had subjected me to. I was always a one-man woman. By sharing my body with a stranger, I knew I would feel a range of emotions that would perhaps would take my focus away from what Kiyan did to me. The rage I was feeling against Kiyan was pushing me to hurt myself. It is deeply insulting to be dumped by the only one person you have in your life and have them be with someone else.

I may have gone to the pub with an agenda but the guts to execute my plan came after I had had four pegs of whisky. My vision was almost starting to blur. I had no clue how I would reach home. I was waiting for the cab I had booked when a guy approached me. I knew he was flirting. I cut him short by asking if he could drop me to my place. He agreed. Once we reached home, I asked if he could open the door for me. The moment he opened the door, he started feeling me up. I wanted to call up Kiyan the way he'd called me, but something made me push away the guy. He stood confused while I tried hard to keep my mind alert. The guy came onto me again. I slapped him. He slapped me. I started howling, punching and kicking him. I think he too punched me since I had bruises this morning. Hearing me howl, he probably must have panicked. He ran away before any other residents woke up. Looking at the mirror, the bruises gave me happiness for it felt like I had punched Kiyan rather than some other guy. Writing about it all, I realized how screwed up the break-up has made me.

The next morning, when I went down for a walk, Kiyan stopped me by the apartment's main gate. He said he wanted to talk. I told him he better. I was eager to know what there was to be told. The unsaid had already said so much. I waited for him to speak up. I was eager to know how he would justify breaking up or if he had some worthy explanation for this decision that had affected me, quite obviously, more deeply than him.

13

Kashti had compelled Kiyan to come three times in a span of nine hours. By the end of it, he had been too tired to even talk. It was like he had been toyed with. He had always been dominating with Anaysha, but with Kashti, being submissive had become a trend by now.

When he woke up in the morning, Kiyan felt claustrophobic in the flat. Kashti was still asleep. He got up, freshened up quickly and then decided to go for a jog to clear his mind. He took one glance at Kashti. The fierceness and the aggression that she had showed last night was quite contradictory to how peacefully she was sleeping right now. She looked like an innocent flower, but Kiyan knew what an erotic thorn she was.

As Kiyan finished jogging two laps around the apartment complex, he doggedly wondered if he could do anything about the situation he was in. When he saw Anaysha leave the building, he stopped. There was a mere five-step distance between them, and yet he knew the metaphorical distance, in the last one week or so, had become immeasurable. He noticed she also stopped.

But then she started brisk walking in the opposite direction. Kiyan knew from the time their engagement had been announced, Anaysha had started walking in the mornings. But had she come down today after she had seen him? He jogged to cover the distance between them and caught up with her. She started walking even faster, but after a point realized Kiyan was intentionally jogging next to her.

'What is it, Kiyan? What do you want from me?' Though she didn't want to be the one to initiate conversation, she had no option. She hadn't known he would come down to jog since he usually went to the gym for his cardio. Well, 'usually' wasn't a word worth relying on any more.

'What happened?' he said, gesturing at a cut on her lips.

'I got hurt,' she said, hoping he would hear the double meaning. She didn't want to tell him about the guy she had brought back from the pub.

Kiyan nervously moistened his lips. He hesitated.

'I'm sorry, Anaysha,' Kiyan said. Both had turned by now to face each other.

'Okay. What next?' Anaysha said, trying her best not to lose her cool.

'It's not how you think it is.'

'Really? Then how is it exactly?'

'I can explain this.'

I thought you'll justify this, Anaysha wondered and said, 'You're still in luck. I'm waiting.'

'I met Kashti during the book events.'

Which means what I thought was right. It was indeed a matter of 9 weeks, Anaysha thought but kept mum, feeling miserable.

'The truth is, I felt insanely attracted towards her. I know I didn't tell you about it, but I don't know why I couldn't.'

During those book events you only met her during the weekends, but you were with me on the weekdays. Were you thinking about her when you were with me? Was my grip on you slowly eroding every weekend when she washed your emotional shores? Or was it mainly sexual? Anaysha wanted to throw these questions at him but was too scared to ask, given how the answers would affect her. There was silence that stemmed out of hesitation. Anaysha didn't ask him to continue. Kiyan kept averting his eyes and then said, 'I slept with her during the book events.'

Anaysha gritted her teeth behind a taut jaw while swallowing a hard lump in her throat. She had guessed it, but hearing it from Kiyan elevated her pain.

'But . . .' he said. And paused because his phone vibrated with a message. He checked it. It had a zoomed-in image of him and Anaysha standing face to face right now and underneath it was written:

Like seriously?

Kiyan rolled his eyes upwards to notice Kashti standing by the window of her flat.

'I'll talk to you later,' Kiyan said and jogged off. Anaysha couldn't believe what had just happened. She kept staring at a disappearing image of Kiyan while Kashti drew the curtain shut.

'So, now you will meet her behind my back, huh?' Kashti asked, opening the door and not letting Kiyan come in.

'It was a chance meeting,' Kiyan said, pushing his way in.

'Chance meeting?'

'I went for a jog. I didn't know I would meet her there.'

'Then what was the need to talk to her?'

'She has injured herself. It's only decent to inquire about it. Anaysha isn't a stranger to me. And for the record, I didn't like the way you clicked a picture of us and sent it to me. It could have been avoided,' Kiyan said and went to sit on the couch. Kashti went up to him and stood behind the couch. She bent down. Her hair fell on his face while she started rubbing her nose against his ears, whispering into his ears, 'I'm sorry baby. Just that it burns me to see you with someone else. I hope you understand that I love you.' She positioned her phone for a selfie and posed, giving him a peck on his cheek. Kiyan smiled casually till the picture was clicked. Immediately after Kashti clicked the selfie, she bit his earlobe softly. Kiyan enjoyed it but didn't make it obvious. He turned around and looked at her.

'I need to bring in my stuff from our flat,' Kiyan said. Looking at Kashti's expression, he realized his mistake.

'I mean Anaysha's flat.'

'Won't it be awkward for you to go back to that flat?'

'Yeah. A little, maybe.'

'Don't worry, baby. I'll do it for you.'

They locked eyes.

'Give me the spare keys,' she said.

'Let Anaysha . . .'

'Do you really need her presence or permission for this?'

Kiyan nodded.

'Just give me the keys.'

Kiyan stood up, went to the bedroom, opened his bag and took out the keys. When he turned around, Kashti was right behind him. She took the keys from him and said, 'Stay right here and chill.'

Kashti took two spare cartons and one of her empty suitcases before locking the main door behind herself. She went to Anaysha's flat. Kiyan was watching through the peephole all the while, hoping Anaysha wouldn't turn up till Kashti was out of the flat. It took Kashti close to thirty minutes to move all of Kiyan's stuff out of the flat. She was about to drag the cartons away when Anaysha stepped out of the elevator.

'Excuse me?' she enquired, looking at the cartons and the suitcases first and then at Kashti.

'Yeah?' Kashti quipped with a I-don't-take-shit-from-anyone attitude.

'If you get into my flat, you have to ask me.'

'But this house also belonged to your ex, who is my boyfriend now.'

Kiyan could hear Kashti's below-the-belt response from behind the door. He was in two minds about opening the door and asking Kashti to come in.

'Your boyfriend doesn't live here any more, so even he needs to take my permission before sending his pet here,' Anaysha stated, holding Kashti's gaze. A fight was on. Kashti kept the suitcase down and looked at Anaysha as if she would slap her. But she smiled in a mocking manner and said, 'I don't blame you. In fact, I feel pity for you. If someone had snatched my boyfriend, I too would have felt this way. The only difference is, nobody can take Kiyan away from me.'

Anaysha was shaking with rage. She wanted to say so much and do so much but couldn't because by then Kiyan had opened the door. He had realized this could turn uglier.

'Let me help with the cartons,' he said, and without looking at either of the girls, picked up one of the cartons and moved it into his new flat with his new partner. Once he had brought in the cartons and the suitcase, he tried to glance at Anaysha. She was already looking at him. Then she banged her main door shut.

'I don't think you should talk to her,' Kiyan told Kashti as he locked their flat door himself.

'I wasn't. She was the one who initiated the conversation.'

'Just ignore her,' he said, knowing well he did so more out of concern for Anaysha than Kashti.

'I'll be more than happy to ignore her.'

'Also, I think we should look for a different place to live,' he said, opening the suitcase.

'We will surely do that, but for the next four months we have to stay here. Dad has paid the rent in advance. I don't think he would like it if I shift before that.'

'Hmm,' Kiyan murmured and kept his focus on the suitcase.

Kashti realized his mood was slightly off. 'Cheer up now,' she said. 'Our selfie fetched two thousand Likes and close to five hundred comments in half an hour.'

Kiyan frowned. He snatched Kashti's phone out of her hand and saw the selfie had been uploaded on his recently made Facebook profile. The caption of the selfie read:

That cozy feeling when you wake up with your love . . .

Kashti had tagged herself on the photograph. The excitement he had seen in Kashti at the Likes and comments disturbed him. And suddenly it dawned on him. Was Kashti trying to feed off his recently acquired fame? Was this entire hunt and game about that four letter word—fame?

14

Kashti had gone out for the day. With some time to think, Kiyan realized he had to move on from the success of his debut trilogy and start working on his next book soon since Natasha had already sent him the contract for it. He knew she had done it intentionally, to bind him to a time frame. He felt uncomfortable working in Kashti's flat. It was too close for comfort to his old flat and brought up memories of when he sat on the bed with the laptop. So Kiyan decided to go to a nearby café and sit there to write.

An author shouldn't rue his or her messy life because it's easy for them to come up with the plot for their next bestseller from that mess. Art often thrives in sadness, angst, anger and chaos. That's why at the back of their minds, authors are always happy about their sadness. And sad when they're happy for too long.

While getting ready to go out, Kiyan kept glancing at the locked wardrobes. He hadn't seen Kashti open them in his presence yet. All her clothes were kept in her bags and suitcases. And yet she told him she had moved in

6 months ago. Who doesn't unpack for this long? Moreover, whenever she left the house, she would lock her bags and suitcases as well. He made a mental note to ask her about it. He was combing his hair in front of the mirror when his phone buzzed with a message from Kashti:

What's up, baby?

Going to a cafe to write, he replied.

Cool. Send me a selfie. My friends here don't believe you are my boyfriend. ☺

Kiyan wondered if his hunch was correct, if she was trying to extract mileage for herself. He stood in front of the mirror in his black T-shirt and clicked a selfie. He sent it to her. The response came immediately.

Muaah. Thanks baby. Black suits you. Have a gorgeous day. See you in the evening.

Kiyan took the spare keys, locked the door and was about to head to the elevator when he was shocked to see Anaysha lying by the main door of her flat. He glanced around but saw nobody. He quickly went to Anaysha, calling out her name, careful not to touch her. She was unconscious. He picked her up in his arms and went inside, placing her on the couch. He went to the kitchen to bring a bottle of water and splashed some water onto her face. Anaysha's eyes opened slightly.

'Anaysha,' Kiyan said, caressing her forehead. The touch brought back a lot of old emotions. He moved his hand. She opened her eyes weakly and then sat up abruptly when she saw it was Kiyan in front of her.

'What happened?' she asked, surprised by his proximity.

'I saw you lying by the door.'

'Oh!' she stood up and went to the kitchen. Kiyan could tell from her gait that everything wasn't all right. He joined her in the kitchen as she drank a glass of water.

'What happened, Anaysha?'

What happened? Really? 'Nothing.' She tapped her fingers against the glass, not knowing what to say or think next. Kiyan kept looking at her.

'I know I went away abruptly yesterday morning . . .' he started but was cut short by Anaysha.

'Not only yesterday morning, Kiyan.' Her tone was acidic. Kiyan lowered his head avoiding eye contact.

'Just leave,' she said. Her hands were shaking now. His presence had the effect of lowering her self-esteem.

'I wanted to tell you . . .' Kiyan started but checked himself when he noticed a security guard at the open door. He rang the bell even though the door was ajar.

'Yes?' Anaysha said.

'Kashti madam sent me to see if everything is okay with you, sir,' the guard said.

'What?' It was so absurd that he didn't understand what the guard meant. He glanced at Anaysha.

'I told you. Just leave, Kiyan,' she said and waited by the main door for him to get out. She locked the door behind him. The guard took the elevator down along with Kiyan. The moment he came out, he called Kashti

162

up. She rejected the call and called him up two minutes later.

'What's this?' he asked.

'What's what?' was the reply.

'Why did you send the guard up?'

'I saw you leaving the flat but not the complex. I inquired, and the guard said the same. He too didn't . . .'

'Wait a minute. What do you mean by you saw me leave the flat?'

There was silence.

'Speak up, Kashti.'

'I have cameras in my flat.'

'What?' Kiyan couldn't keep the disbelief out of his voice.

'I have a live feed on my phone. Don't be angry. It's because I want to see you all the time. I miss you a lot.'

Kiyan kept quiet.

'Kiyan, you there?'

'Yeah,' he said and wondered about what she said. *She installed hidden cameras because she misses him? Who does that sort of thing?*

'Message me from the cafe. You're going there now, right?' she asked.

'Right.'

There was a limit to possessiveness. And Kashti had reached it with her behaviour. Or so Kiyan thought.

He sat at the Starbucks in Cyber Hub for a good five hours. And for all his effort, he had a blank page.

He simply couldn't focus. More so because he was trying to write his next story about a character based on Kashti. The real and fictitious worlds were colliding, and he ended up going over the book events, the gym in Bangalore, Sarafa in Indore and the beach in Goa. Initially, Kashti was a mystery he was eager to unveil, but now the same mystery was scaring him. Had it not been for the 'gift' she had given him it wouldn't have led to this.

Kiyan also couldn't stop thinking about Anaysha lying on the floor like that. He kept staring at her number on his phone, debating whether he should call and ask her.

As he was trying to gather courage, he heard someone say, 'Hey Kiyan!' It was his editor, Natasha.

'Hey!'

'What a surprise! Please tell me you are working on your next here.'

Kiyan turned his laptop towards her and said, 'Yeah, wrote a lot.' Natasha noticed all that was written on the page was the word 'PROLOGUE'.

'Hmm, give me fifteen minutes. I have a quick meeting to finish. Then let's sit over coffee,' she said.

'Sure, I'm here.'

Natasha joined him twenty minutes later, carrying a Red Velvet Frappé.

'So, what's the problem?' she asked, sitting opposite him.

'I'm stuck.' Only Kiyan knew he wasn't talking about his writing.

'It happens to every author, especially with the second project. But trust me, it'll pass. You just need one instance of inspiration.'

'And I'm that instance of inspiration for Kiyan.'

Both Natasha and Kiyan turned around to see Kashti beaming at them. After a moment's awkwardness, Kiyan stood up and introduced Kashti to Natasha as his girlfriend.

'I saw your pictures on Kiyan's profile and page.' Natasha said, giving Kashti a one-shoulder hug. Kashti hugged Kiyan tightly once and took her seat.

'What do you want to have?' Natasha asked.

'I already have what I want,' Kashti said with a sly smile, holding Kiyan's hand and squeezing it tightly.

'Of course,' Natasha said, letting it show on her face that she found the display of possession a little weird.

'Anyway, I'll order something to drink,' Kashti said.

'Let me,' Kiyan said, but Kashti stopped him saying, 'It's okay, hon.'

As Kashti went to the counter to order, Natasha turned to Kiyan and said, 'She loves you a lot.'

Kiyan didn't miss the sarcasm 'a lot' was laced with. He nodded.

'Where did you meet her?'

'At a cousin's wedding.' He couldn't bring himself to tell the truth.

'And how long have you been in the relationship?'

'A few months.'

'Nice,' Natasha said.

Kiyan acknowledged the comment with a smile, knowing well what she was hinting at. Kashti joined them soon enough. They chatted about nothing in particular for some time, after which Natasha took her leave.

'How did you know I was here?' Kiyan asked Kashti right after waving at Natasha.

'Someone told me.'

'Who?'

'What's this with your interrogation?'

'Just answer me, Kashti.'

'All right. A friend of mine spotted you here. I never told you, but all my friends have a crush on you. And they are jealous of me because they read your books and always keep fangirling while I have you for real.' She had a condescending smirk on her face.

'So a friend of yours spotted me here and told you about it, and you came here?'

'To surprise you.'

'I don't like it, Kashti. This and the cameras.'

'I told you I installed them so that I can see you every time I miss you. I can't always ask you to click a selfie. Why are you getting so bothered about it?'

'I don't like to be watched. That's all.'

'That's why I didn't want to tell you about it. Okay I shall remove them, happy?'

'Yeah, fine.'

'Well, let me tell you something. One of your fans made a page for us,' Kashti said.

'Us?'

'Yeah. Look.' She showed him a Facebook page on her phone and said, 'The fan made me the admin. How sweet, no? And guess what, we already have 5,000 Likes in a span of 9 hours. And just look at the posts they have put up. They want to see more of us. We are their dream couple.'

Kiyan checked the posts as Kashti slowly scrolled down the page on her phone. Most of them were demands from readers to post more pictures and videos, and compliments about how perfect they looked together.

'You have to look at our last kissing picture that I put up. The girls are getting jealous. I like that. It's a kick you know, of the ultimate kind. The guy they fantasize about, I get to tie him up and savour him,' she said with a smile. If he was the person who had obsessed about Kashti during the book tour, he would thought the smile was alluring, but now the smile made him think she was perhaps crazy.

She closed the Facebook app on her phone and turned to Kiyan with a serious face.

'Tell me, what were you doing at Anaysha's flat in the morning?'

'She was lying unconscious and . . .'

'Give me your phone.'

Kiyan gave her his phone. She blocked Anaysha on Whatsapp and then deleted her number from his contact list.

'What are you doing?'

'Don't you get it, Kiyan? She is trying to win you back from me. What do you think, coming out in the morning when you are jogging and lying unconscious on the floor when you are about to leave the flat are coincidences? I'm a girl, and I know how girls are.'

Kiyan was lost in thought.

'But that's not important. What's important is whether you would let her win you back?' she asked, looking deep into his eyes. The same way she had looked at him after she had given him the 'gift' in Goa.

All Kiyan could do was nod slowly, which made Kashti give him a peck and say, 'That's like my baby.'

15

The first thing Kiyan did after they reached their flat was to remove all the hidden cameras with Kashti's help. He was surprised by the number of them. There were ten in all—in the bedroom, drawing room, kitchen, washroom and balcony. The entire flat was under survelliance, and only Kashti had access to the live feed on her phone.

'When did you install them?'

'A day before your Indore launch.'

The confidence with which she said it told Kiyan how easy all of it had been. If he wrote about this in his next book, readers would ask how an author could fall so easily for Kashti. But truth is always stranger than fiction.

Though she promised him there were no more cameras in the flat, Kiyan wasn't sure. Not that he had any option other than to believe her. The fact that he had sat for five hours straight at Starbucks earlier in the day but hadn't written one word disturbed him deeply. He knew it couldn't go on like this. He would have to submit the manuscript in the next five months and for that he would have to start immediately. And before starting, he had to take care of the reason he couldn't focus. The reason was sleeping beside him in a white, semi-transparent, V-neck T-shirt that had ridden up her stomach while sleeping, with her tiny belly button showing. The outline of her nipples on her T-shirt told him she wasn't wearing a bra. She was wearing no pants and had on a white panty. He gazed at her shapely legs and wondered what apart from her body was alluring to him. What else did he know about her? Her name. Her address. Her phone number. Her daily routine. Her parents were in the US. She had an elder sister. That's it. A sinking feeling in his gut made Kiyan sit up in bed. He knew why he had chosen her over Anaysha. It was because of the 'gift' Kashti had given him in Goa. But he couldn't live like this for ever. He glanced at her face. She wasn't the kind of girl anyone could live with. She was way too dominating, too intrusive and too possessive. In fact, she was the opposite of Anaysha. For a moment, Kiyan felt like crying. He knew he shouldn't have slipped up in the gym in Bangalore, or more importantly, at the beach in Goa. People give in to temptations not solely because of what they offer but also because of a larger reason that surfaces from within when the temptation comes along. If not with Kashti, he would have been tempted by someone else sooner or later. The problem was that this temptation called Kashti was a fatal one.

Kiyan only wished he had known about it in time. Now it was too late. Or was it?

Kiyan wanted to go over to Anaysha right at that moment, hug her tightly and apologize. But he knew he wouldn't be able to. He closed his eyes and tried to focus. First things first—to get out of any trap, one has to first understand the trap in its totality. Kiyan recollected that Kashti had told him the user ID and password for the Facebook profile. He downloaded the Facebook app on his phone, and for the first time since college, logged on. The profile was in his name. He soon discovered that he was the admin for both his and Kashti's fan page as well. Why exactly were people her fan? Because she was *his* girlfriend? Kiyan Roy's girlfriend! He couldn't help but smirk. He soon found Kashti's profile too in his friend list. The profile picture was of her in the same clothes she had worn at the lounge in Pune.

Kiyan looked through her friends to try to find more information. He noticed there were 857 people in her friends list, but none of them seemed like they might be her friend. For one, they were all middle-aged, weird-looking males. Secondly, none of the ten pictures she had uploaded had any comment from a female. The Likes, shares and comments were all by lecherous-looking males. Was that normal? Though he wasn't familiar with social media he knew it was a medium to connect with friends, keep track of what was happening in their lives and let them know about your own. He typed Anaysha

Gupta in the search bar. However, no search result showed up. Anaysha wasn't very social media friendly, like him, though she did have a profile. As he lifted his head up from the phone, wondering how else he could know more about Kashti without making it obvious to her, his eyes fell on the locked wardrobe.

Kashti went out the next morning around her usual time, 8 a.m. Kiyan acted sleepy when she left. When he heard the door lock, Kiyan immediately went to the kitchen. Behind the door was a small shelf he had discovered the day he had shifted. Kashti kept all kinds of things there, including a small hammer. He picked it up and went straight to the wardrobe in Kashti's room. He took a picture of the tiny lock with his phone so that he could replace it later with an identical lock. With one blow, he broke the lock in half. Kiyan opened the wardrobe to find it totally empty, except for a file. He took out the file and opened it. There were a few documents inside, including a medical prescription. But the patient name wasn't Kashti. The name made him frown.

16

Tina Awasthi.

Kiyan read the name of the patient on the prescription again. He couldn't believe it. Was it the same Tina he had met while doing research for *Handcuffs*? The one who had inspired it? But she never had any mental illness. And what was her prescription doing in Kashti's cupboard? He quickly took out his phone, clicked a picture of the prescription and checked for Tina's number on his contact list. He had no contact under the alphabet T. Kiyan remembered he had changed his phone a year ago and lost some contacts. Since then, he had never had Tina's number. As he stood by the cupboard, wondering, his phone rang. It was Kashti. He picked up.

'Hey baby. Our morning always goes by in a rush. I just reached. What's your plan for the day?'

Go look for Tina first at her place and then figure out how you know her, Kiyan thought and said, 'Nothing much. Will probably go to some café and write.'

'Great. I'll come home and read whatever you write,' she said, as if she was his mom who wanted to check her child's homework.

'Sure,' he said nonchalantly and hung up.

Kiyan took a quick shower, finished the breakfast that Kashti had made for him and left for Tina's place. He had last met her in her flat in Lajpat Nagar. He took the Metro and reached Lajpat Nagar an hour and a half later. Tina's apartment was a five-minute walk away from the Metro station. The security guard beamed at him. He responded with a tight smile. He took the elevator and went to the second floor. The prescription in Tina's name couldn't be a coincidence. Kashti had to be connected to her in some way. But why had she kept it a secret from him? The elevator stopped, and Kiyan headed for Tina's flat, when he heard a voice, 'She isn't there.'

Kiyan turned around to see the old neighbour he had always exchanged a smile with whenever he used to visit Tina. The old lady was handing over some clothes to a laundry boy.

'Tina isn't here?' he asked.

'I don't know. I haven't seen her of late. I think she has shifted.'

Kiyan stared at the locked door. Waiting seemed futile, so he decided to leave.

'You have come here after a long time,' the old lady remarked. She always had an I-know-what-you-are-up-to smile on her face that made Kiyan uncomfortable.

'Yeah, I was busy. Take care,' he said and took the stairs down. He was wondering how he could track Tina, and if it was even necessary to do so, when he froze. Kashti was standing by the entrance of the building.

'What are you doing here?' he said, not able to hide his amazement.

'Don't use my line. I want to know what you are doing here.'

'Wait. How did you know I was here?'

'I know your Apple ID. So I tracked your iPhone. When I realized you weren't in a cafe as you said you would be, I came here. Moreover . . .'

Kiyan waited for her to finish even though he couldn't fathom how ridiculous it was for this girl to keep following him around.

'This is where my sister used to live.'

'Your sister?'

'Tina Awasthi is my elder sister. I'm Kashti Awasthi.'

'Where is she now?'

'I told you, she is in the US with my parents.' A pause later she added, 'She is undergoing a check-up for mental illness.'

'What for?'

'Some guy shit. He betrayed her. And she couldn't take it.'

Kiyan swallowed a lump in his throat. He knew who the guy was. But the question was—did anyone else know?

'Now tell me, Kiyan, what are you doing here?' Kashti asked. Kiyan knew he had little less than a few seconds to conjure up a story.

17

'An old friend used to live here,' Kiyan blurted out.

'Used to?' Kashti frowned and said, 'Then why are you here?'

'I got to know only now.'

'Oh. You could have called him . . . or is it a her?' The last part came out quite threateningly.

'Him.'

'Okay. What's his name? I may know him.'

'Forget it. It's not important.' Kiyan said and started walking away, followed by Kashti. He stopped suddenly, struck by the thought that he had never seen Kashti when he had visited Tina. *Moreover, she never told me she had a younger sister.*

'Funny we never met even though I used to visit often and you lived here.' That was the best way Kiyan could think of to frame his original thought.

'Who told you I lived here? I was in a boarding school in Dehradun.'

'Okay,' he said, not willing to believe her.

'Let's take the Metro home.'

Kiyan was quiet for most of the journey while Kashti was busy replying to his fans whose messages had poured in on their couple page on Facebook. While he kept glancing at her from time to time, he tried to decide if Tina's relation to Kashti was just a coincidence

'Where did you say your parents were?'

'Huh?' Kashti seemed taken aback. Kiyan repeated himself.

'They are in the US.'

'Where in the US?'

'Atlanta.'

'Is it because . . .'

Kashti nodded and replied before Kiyan could complete, 'It's because of my sister's treatment.'

'What exactly has happened to her?'

'The fact that the guy betrayed her simply got to her. It was too traumatic for her.'

'Didn't your parents find out who the guy was?' Kiyan asked casually, trying to put across the question in a thoughtful manner.

Kashti gave him a sharp glance and said, 'They tried, but in vain. Tina Di literally turned dumb.'

Kiyan was yet again lost in thought when he felt Kashti's hands around him and her head on his shoulder.

'I feel so lonely at times, Kiyan. I know you must be wondering why I'm so possessive. My previous boyfriend also thought like that and left me.'

Is that why you gave me that 'gift', so that I don't ever leave you? Kiyan thought and heard Kashti continue, 'Even my parents kept me in a boarding school from the beginning because they thought I was difficult. Maybe staying alone has made me so particular about the things I like, love,' she said and hugged him closer.

'But now I have you,' she said and kissed him on his neck.

PDA had never been Kiyan's thing. His discomfort was evident as he glanced at the people in the Metro looking at them.

'Kashti, people are looking,' he whispered. She looked up at him and kissed him right on his lips.

'Do you think I give a fuck?' she asked and winked at him. Kiyan didn't know where to look. He simply unlocked his phone and stared at it.

Once they reached Gurgaon, Kiyan excused himself to go to a café to write while Kashti went to their flat. Taking cues from what was happening around him, a new plot assembled itself in his mind. What if a girl's younger sister approached a bestselling author as his fan to avenge her sister and punish the author who left the sister? The thought excited Kiyan, and he immediately wrote a one-page synopsis and mailed it to Natasha. After a long time, the author in him was happy. To use one's reality as a trigger to knit a fictional tale is an innate talent. Everyone believes that authors are creative people, but Kiyan's own experience had taught him that authors are experts at recycling. He left the café the moment Natasha messaged him that she had received the synopsis and would reply over the weekend.

Use your key. I'm in the shower. Kiyan read Kashti's message for him on his way home. Before unlocking the door to Kashti's flat, he glanced at Anaysha's door and noticed a lock on it. He pushed open the door, calling out to Kashti, but there was no response. Instead, he heard moans and grunts. He became alert and noticed Kashti's laptop was on. A video of one of their sexual escapades in Goa was playing. He was about to call out to Kashti again when he heard her voice. He followed it to the bedroom. He saw Kashti, wrapped in a towel, drying her hair with a dryer by the mirror and talking on the phone with her back to him.

'I'm not sure, but I think he has his doubts. Why else would he visit her apartment? No, he hasn't come home yet.'

Kiyan felt his heart thudding. His doubt seemed to have been correct. He thought back to the time Kashti had come into his life, from the photographs to the pub dance and the gym in Bangalore to the beach in Goa. He started walking backwards and slowly exited the flat. With shaking hands, he pressed the elevator button. It was on the same floor. He pressed the ground floor button, and the moment the door closed, Kiyan felt weak in his knees. He slid to the floor with tears in his eyes. It was a game of revenge. Looking at the gift he had correctly guessed she must have recorded their escapades. And she had. He held his head and was about to break down when the elevator reached the ground floor. The doors opened. He saw a pair of sandal-encased feet enter the lift.

'What happened?' It was Anaysha.

Kiyan looked up at her. And started crying like a baby.

* * *

Anaysha's Diary

Finally, I know why Kiyan broke up with me. I didn't know how to react when I found him wailing in the elevator. He said he wanted to talk. I hadn't seen him like this ever. I thought of avoiding him but I couldn't. We went to the emergency exit stairwell of our building, which was quite secluded. I had some water with me. After he had gulped some down, he relaxed. Then he told me how Kashti had lured him during the book tour. In Bangalore they hadn't had sex, but in Goa they did . . . by the beach. It was always my fantasy . . . to do Kiyan by the beach on our honeymoon. Hearing he had done it with someone else made my mind go blank. I controlled myself somehow as he told me how Kashti had taken him to her shack on the beach and gifted him something. Even Kiyan was surprised by it. He unwrapped it to find Kashti's birth certificate. Initially he thought it was her way of telling him it was her birthday since it was 20 March. But then she asked him to look at the year. 1999. It was then that Kiyan understood what a mess he was in. He had had sex with a fucking underage girl! Sex with a minor is a punishable offence. It would destroy his career and reputation forever. And of course, Kashti had recorded their beach sex in night mode on her DSLR.

Kashti's first demand was that he would have to call off our engagement and abandon me. Kiyan really had no options. Finally, I could understand everything, but I was hurt that he hadn't even tried to tell me the real reason. I would have cancelled the engagement myself with some excuse, and we would have dealt with the situation together. He had nothing to say. He did what he thought was best—to keep quiet and follow Kashti's 'demands'. All she wanted was Kiyan. Wiping his tears, he went up to his flat. Though I felt bad that he had fallen for Kashti's charms, my heart went out to him in his present condition. It disturbed me and told me he needed me.

Since I had heard Kiyan confess, my heart had been asking me only one thing—*can you trust him?* Can't a person who weaves stories for a living simply weave another one only to appease me? But why would he appease me now? Unless he needed me by his side for something. There's no way I'll ever know if he told me the truth this evening. His confession did make me realize that lust really can lead someone astray. What I want to know is if love can win the same person back.

Part 3: Destroy

18

Kiyan had gone back to his flat after talking to Anaysha. Sharing his feelings had made him feel lighter. And he only hoped Anaysha understood why he had called off the engagement. He had been forced to. Kiyan wasn't a child who hadn't understood what Kashti had implied when she gifted him the birth certificate. Once he was with Kashti in their flat, he didn't know what to talk about, what to ask and how to behave. Should he ask her outright what was she up to? Was trapping him with her birth certificate the first step to whatever she was up to? It was certainly not what she had told him earlier. She had boldly told him in Goa after giving him her birth certificate, 'I did this to keep you bound to me. I'm an acutely insecure and fiercely possessive girl, Kiyan. And that can make me a difficult girlfriend, I know, but also an amazing lover, which you will come to know soon.'

Now he knew it wasn't just that. There was more to the story. Kiyan behaved as normally as he could with Kashti over dinner. When she fell asleep, he tried to guess Kashti's phone password and check who she had been talking to earlier in the evening, but had no luck. Disappointed, he returned the phone to its place beside her pillow.

In the morning once she went to school, in Noida, Kiyan went to Starbucks in Cyber Hub to think through his next step. He was a caged animal who could only pace the perimeter he was fenced into. After ordering himself a frappé, Kiyan sat down in a corner inside Starbucks. For the next few minutes, he tried hard but couldn't surmise what Kashti's agenda was to have trapped him like this. The best answer (apart from the obvious but not plausible one of revenge) he could come up with was that Kashti coveted his fame. Fame was a drug for today's youngsters. And it is the only drug that alters moral and emotional fibres even before a person has had a taste of it. How could she really be Tina's sister? He had never heard her mention Kashti at all.

Kiyan's musing was interrupted when someone set down a cappuccino on his table. He looked up and saw Anaysha. Though he had thought of messaging her after his outburst in the stairwell, he was sure he didn't have the right to request her to be his emotional solace any more. She took a seat beside him.

'I followed Kashti to her school today,' she said. Kiyan couldn't hide his incredulity.

'The bad thing is, she is indeed in school, which means her birth certificate is genuine. She is underage. And she can take you to the police any time.'

The fact Anaysha still cared made him feel worse about himself and his behaviour. 'I know, that's why I . . .' Kiyan knew Anaysha would understand the rest of it.

Neither spoke. Kiyan didn't know what exactly he should say first—sorry or all the other things that he wanted to say. On the other hand, Anaysha didn't know what to ask first—what were you doing sleeping with an underage girl or why did you sleep with anyone in the first place when you were in a relationship with me?

'I'm sorry,' Kiyan said. His eyes and expression showed he really meant it. Anaysha didn't say a word. She simply mixed the brown sugar in her cappuccino and took a sip. Then she pushed the cappuccino towards him.

'Can you take the sugar out of this coffee?' she asked. Kiyan glanced at her as she continued stirring the cappuccino. He understood her point. Some things couldn't be undone. He remained quiet.

'I followed Kashti today because I can't see you like this. Trapped. It may surprise you because you haven't loved me the way I have loved you,' she said.

'I . . .' Kiyan started, moistened his dry lips and continued with awkwardness, 'I can't even say it was a mistake because it wasn't. I chose to sleep with her. I chose to cheat on you. I chose to . . .'

'Kiyan, I'm not trying to help you realize how great my love was for you or make you feel pathetic for cheating on me. I just want to help you this one final time because I know I won't be able to rest in peace now that I know what made you break off our engagement. Once I help you get rid of Kashti, I shall be out of your life forever.'

'But I need you.'

They looked into each other's eyes for a moment.

'Don't say that again,' she said threateningly but didn't look away. Kiyan's name was called at the counter. He fetched his frappé. Once he had taken his seat again, Anaysha said, 'I only have one question for you. What if Kashti had not given you the birth certificate? What if she had not trapped you the way she has? Would you have told me about your dalliance or would you have quietly married me, saying 'I love you' the way you did before Kashti happened to you?'

Kiyan knew the answer. Hence he couldn't say it aloud. After a few seconds of silence, Anaysha too knew the answer and didn't wait for him to speak.

'Yesterday you told me you found another girl's medical prescription in the cupboard?' Anaysha asked.

Kiyan nodded.

'Is the girl related to Kashti?'

Kiyan took few seconds before he said, 'I don't know. Kashti said she is her sister.'

'What's her name?'

'Tina Awasthi.'

'You know her?'

Kiyan nodded.

'Who is Tina Awasthi? I have never heard this name before,' Anaysha said.

'She used to work in a software MNC in Cyber City. We met via a common friend. And . . .' A pause and an eye lock later he added, 'She wanted to marry me. She was mad about me.'

'When was this?'

'Been a year and a half.'

'And then?'

'I told her I was committed, but she simply couldn't accept the fact. Then one day she stopped coming to office. I tried to check if she was okay, but her number wasn't working. I haven't met or heard anything about her since till I saw her name on the psychiatrist's prescription in Kashti's cupboard. She told me Tina is being treated in the US since she is mentally ill.'

'And the reason for that?'

'A guy. That's what Kashti said. She doesn't know who the guy is. I am not sure if she's lying about that.'

'I'm sure she is. This can't be a coincidence. You'll have to extract more information from her, Kiyan. The more I think about it, the more possible it seems. A younger sister who thinks the guy is to be blamed for her elder sister's condition gets in touch with him and avenges her sister.'

'But why would she keep me captive like this? Why not confront me?' Kiyan said.

A pause later Anaysha said, 'I'm sure she is bluffing about not knowing the guy her sister was madly in love with was you.'

'But how can we be sure of it?' Kiyan asked. He had thought of the revenge angle, but the fact that he hadn't heard about Kashti from Tina was making him think it wasn't the only possible reason for Kashti's appearance in his life.

'The way she trapped you—seduction.' Anaysha said.

Kiyan kept looking at Anaysha till he was sure she had meant what she had said.

'But she is only 17.'

'You have to choose, Kiyan. Do you want to get out of this mess or do you want to be morally correct? Don't forget that this 17-year-old trapped you to begin with,' she said. Kiyan thought about it. Kashti was physically 17, but her mind was that of an adult. An evil adult. Kashti's evilness made him look around to check if someone was watching them. Nobody was.

'I get your point,' he said, looking straight at Anaysha.

Kiyan got home from Starbucks before Kashti did. She rang the doorbell, but when Kiyan didn't open the door, she used her spare key.

'I know you are at home, baby. The phone tracker tells me so. You don't have to surprise . . .' She walked through the house looking for him and paused mid-sentence when she opened the bathroom door. A lot of empty beer bottles were kept to one side. She glanced at the bathtub, which was filled to the brim with beer and had a couple of condoms on the rim. She felt two hands grab her waist. She closed her eyes as Kiyan turned her around. He had gulped a mouthful of chilled beer, which he slowly released on her forehead. As the beer trickled down her face, goosebumps appeared on her flesh. Kiyan started licking the beer off her. His hands were quick to unbuckle her belt and unhook her skirt. They fell to the ground. As he unbuttoned her shirt, she took off her socks using her feet. As he untucked her shirt, keeping the tie on, she unhooked her bra. Kiyan slowly tightened the knot and said, 'I missed you very much today.' He was wearing only a pair of black briefs. As she caressed his abs with her fingertips, he loosened the tie and pulled it over her head. He cupped her face with both hands and kissed her hard and deep, exploring her mouth. She put her hands inside his briefs on his bare butt, squeezed them once and tugged the briefs down. As the smooch continued, Kiyan took off the briefs while gently pushing her backwards till her legs hit the bathtub.

'I want to know more about you, baby,' Kiyan said in a rasping voice.

'You are most welcome to,' Kashti said.

Both of them got into the bathtub, still smooching. Kiyan made her lie down and got on top. The beer was chilled. Kashti felt goosebumps all over her body. Her breathing quickened, and she drew Kiyan closer to her for warmth. She felt his tongue lick the beer off every inch of her body. Her eyes rolled back when he started sucking on her toes, kissed his way to her calf muscles and bit her hard. It was the first time he was taking the lead during sex. Kashti liked the unexpected role reversal. Though Kiyan was hesitating to enter her, Kashti held his erect penis, rolled on one of the condoms kept on the rim and guided it to her vagina. The friction numbed Kiyan's mind. He pushed it inside. A prolonged moan escaped Kashti. She moved her pelvis as she put her hands around his waist. They looked deep into each other's eyes as Kiyan asked, 'Is there anything you are hiding from me, Kashti?'

She responded after few seconds, 'Why would I hide anything from you?'

'You tell me.'

'I won't hide anything from you. Come on, harder now.'

Kiyan started thrusting even faster and deeper, knowing it was a lie.

'You are lying?'

'I'm not lying. Faster, Kiyan!'

Kiyan increased his speed as well as force. As his eyes started rolling backwards with pleasure, he realized the pleasure zenith was coming soon.

'Is it just a coincidence that you approached me at the New Delhi book event?' he whispered in her ears as he felt her grip on his hips tighten.

'Yes . . . everything . . . is . . . a . . . coincidence. Harder Kiyan . . . do me harder . . . like I'm your fuck slave.'

Her nails were slowly digging into his flesh as beer kept spilling over the bathtub. He had never fucked her this hard. It was on the verge of pain, but all Kashti could feel was pleasure. Their copulation reached a crescendo in the next few seconds.

'Tell me . . .' Even Kiyan's release was close.

'What . . .' she knew her muscles would spasm any moment.

'What is it? I know there's something.'

'Who told you?'

'Instinct.'

'I want to avenge what you did to my sister.'

'Who . . . is . . . the . . . guy?'

'I . . . don't . . . know . . . yet.'

They came together. As their breathing returned to normal, Kashti looked at Kiyan and said, 'Would you help me get to the guy?'

Kiyan stole a glance at her and then buried his face in her soft bosom.

19

The next morning, Kiyan was still in bed when Kashti got ready and left for school. He knew he had to get in touch with Anaysha, but he didn't want Kashti to get to know about it. He left the flat at his usual time and went to the same Starbucks he had been frequenting. He was hoping Anaysha would meet him there on her own the way she did the other day. She didn't disappoint him.

'I was right behind you,' she said, moving towards the seat across him. Kiyan looked over her shoulder and then at Anaysha, and said, 'Sorry, do I know you?'

Anaysha frowned but when her eyes met his, she understood something was wrong. She apologized and went to another table. Kiyan had noticed a teenage girl staring at him through the glass wall, sitting right outside Starbucks. As Anaysha went away, the girl stood up and came inside, to where Kiyan was sitting. He had a feeling she was one of Kashti's friends. He was going to make sure Kashti didn't know he was meeting Anaysha yet again.

'You are Kiyan Roy, right?' she said.

'Yes.'

'I'm a big fan. Can I get a selfie with you please?'

Kiyan relaxed. He stood up and posed for a selfie with the girl. She thanked him, praised his trilogy and told him she was waiting for his next book. *Next book?* Kiyan knew he would write the next book only when he was done with Kashti.

The girl went away checking the selfie on her phone while Kiyan joined Anaysha at her table.

'Sorry. I thought it was one of Kashti's friends.'

'I understood that. But do you know any of her friends?' Anaysha asked.

'I don't. I checked her Facebook profile, but none of them seemed like her true friends.'

'She's clearly hiding a lot of things. And we need to get to the bottom of it before it is too late,' Anaysha said.

'Too late?'

'Obviously she has an agenda. She has a plan.' *Separating us was a part of that plan*, she thought.

'Hmmm.'

'By the way, did you get her to confess anything last night?'

'I tried, but . . .'

I tried . . . Anaysha knew what he meant by that. He must have seduced her. She remembered how she had been made to hear them having sex. Now she knew it must have been Kashti's ploy to make Anaysha realize she had lost Kiyan to her. Anaysha sighed, thinking about the last time Kiyan and she had made love, before he left Delhi for his first book event. It had been more than two months ago. She knew how good a lover he could be. Suddenly, with him sitting before her, she wondered why this couldn't be like old times. Why did life have to make it so complicated? She craved for him emotionally but couldn't confess her urges. She felt like his name was still etched into her heart. And yet . . .

'What happened?' Kiyan nudged her gently.

Anaysha nodded and said, 'Should we go somewhere else? People may recognize you here.'

'Actually, Kashti tracks my phone. She will know if I'm not in Starbucks.'

'Tracks your phone? How?'

Kiyan explained how an iPhone can be traced if someone accessed the phone's Apple ID.

'But don't you need a password to log in to the ID?'

'Yes, but Kashti somehow guessed the password. It wasn't that difficult after all.'

'What is the password?'

'Kiyananaysha30.'

30 was Anaysha's birth date. Hearing their names together sounded like listening to a eulogy of their relationship.

She thought for some time and said, 'She can track your phone. Not you. Let's keep the phone with Rahul and go somewhere else.'

'Who's Rahul?'

'He works here. Once he saw me reading a book and recommended something that I loved. Since then, we keep recommending books to each other. You can say that he is my book buddy.'

'Okay. But what if Kashti calls up?'

'You can always tell her you kept it on silent mode to focus on work. And I'll tell Rahul to inform me if anyone calls on your phone.'

'Sounds neat. I'm sick and tired of her controlling nature,' he said and stood up.

The statement made Anaysha feel good about herself, even though she knew it hadn't been Kiyan's objective of saying it. She gave Kiyan's phone to Rahul and together they exited Starbucks.

They took an Ola cab and gave the driver a nearby destination they had no intention of going to. It seemed to be a better idea to discuss their plan in a moving car, without risk of being watched or interrupted. Later, they could ask the cab to turn around and take them back to Starbucks.

'Last night, she asked me if I would help her find the guy who rejected Tina,' Kiyan said, turning sideways to look at Anaysha.

'What did you say?'

'I said okay.'

'What do you think? Is she telling the truth?'

'I don't know. But she is definitely hiding something.'

'What makes you so sure?'

'The phone call she made that day seemed really suspicious. Also, her locked cupboards? I mean who keeps their cupboards locked and clothes in a bag, even after living there for 6 months? In fact, I'm yet to meet her local guardians.'

'Local guardians?'

'She told me her uncle is her local guardian. But I don't know the exact address.' A pause later he added, 'What should we do now?'

Could this attempt of hers to rescue Kiyan from the crisis bring them close again? Anaysha wondered. She had told him clearly she would leave him forever once the Kashti issue was sorted, but what if by then she discovered the old Kiyan once again? Did that kind of thing happen to people? First falling in love, then separating and then again coming together?

'My next book is suffering. I'm not able to focus at all,' Kiyan lamented.

'There is only one way to know if she is playing smart or whether she really doesn't know about the guy responsible for Tina's condition. If Kashti already knows it's you then she is asking you for help only to buy time to finish whatever she has in mind. But if she seriously doesn't know you are the guy, then . . .'

The cab went over a bumpy speedbreaker, forcing her to pause.

'Then?' he egged her on.

'Then you should ask her how to find the guy. It might tell us just how much she knows.'

Kiyan mulled over Anaysha's plan.

'Bhaiya, Cyber Hub wapas le lo.' Kiyan said to the driver, punching in the new destination on the Ola app on Anaysha's phone, and turned to Anaysha to say, 'You are right. If she wants to find that guy then let me help her reach him. If it is me or someone else I will know soon, and along with it, what exactly she has in mind for the guy.'

'Right!'

The Ola cab drove them back to Cyber Hub. Anaysha went to her office while Kiyan collected his phone from Rahul and went home. He waited for Kashti. When the doorbell finally rang a tad before her usual time of arrival, Kiyan was quick to open the door. He had his queries framed perfectly in his head and also the perfect time to ask them—when they were drinking their evening coffee. But Kiyan opened the door to see Kashti looking like he had never seen her before. She was crying.

'What happened?' he gasped.

Kashti hugged him tightly and said in a whimpering voice, 'Tina Di committed suicide last night.'

Kiyan frowned as he caressed her back, trying to calm her down.

'I won't leave the bastard. I swear,' she said. Kiyan swallowed a lump in his throat. He asked, 'Do you now know who the guy is?'

20

Kashti was on the bed, cuddled in Kiyan's arms. They had skipped dinner. She didn't feel like eating, while Kiyan had only his protein shake. When he had asked her if she knew who the boy was, she had replied no.

Lying in bed with her head on his chest, Kashti had her eyes closed, with dried tears on her cheeks. Kiyan had had to console her for more than an hour before she stopped crying.

'Tell me what happened.'

'She consumed poison last night. Mom and Dad found her dead some time later.'

'Just like that?'

'Not just like that. I told you she was disturbed because of that bastard who broke her heart.'

Kiyan stopped probing further. Lost in thought he caressed her bare back. She had put his hand inside her T-shirt, saying it made her feel peaceful. With his fingers moving gently over her skin, she looked up and said, 'Aren't you sleepy?'

Kiyan nodded and said, 'What exactly happened between your sister and the guy?'

'She loved him but he played with her.'

'Played with her?' he asked.

'Yes. Toyed with her emotions. Left her suddenly.'

'Are you sure?'

'What do you mean?'

'I mean,' Kiyan chose his words carefully and said, 'You don't know the guy but have already judged him?'

Kashti sat up, moving away from his grasp, 'My sister killed herself because of him, Kiyan. I think I have enough reasons to judge him.' Kiyan understood this was going the other way, where he hadn't intended it to.

'Calm down.' He put his hands on her waist and pulled her towards him. Looking into her eyes he said, 'How do we get to this guy?'

Kashti stared at him and then smiled, saying, 'Thanks for the support, baby.' She put her head back on his chest and said, 'I don't know how. By the time I knew what had happened with Tina Di, she had already become unbalanced. I didn't even hear her say his name ever. Moreover, I have stayed in a boarding school for most of my childhood, so I was always away from her. And yet I loved her so much . . .' She started sobbing again.

'Calm down, Kashti. I know it's a difficult time, but nothing can be done now.'

Kashti's phone rang. It was on the bedside table close to Kiyan. He picked it up, glanced at the screen casually and saw 'Mom' written on it. This was the first time he had seen Kashti's mother call her. He gave the phone to her.

'Yeah, Mom.' As she talked, Kiyan was lost in thought. What if her parents knew something about the guy? For a moment, he put himself in Kashti's shoes. What would he have done if he came to know his sister went crazy and committed suicide because of a guy he had by the balls? He shuddered at the answer that popped into his head.

'I'm leaving for the US tomorrow night,' Kashti said, throwing the phone down on the bed.

'Aren't they bringing the body here?'

'No. I will shift to the US after my boards. My parents have decided to settle there now. I was the only connection to India for them anyway.'

And all I'm hoping for is that you don't come to know the name of the guy till you shift to the US, Kiyan thought and said, 'I see.'

'You will also shift with me,' Kashti said, hugging him.

'I wish, but you know I'll have to be here for my work.'

'What's the problem? You can write from the US and email your publisher whatever they need. Then we can come here together for promotions.'

'I write stories for Indians, and for that I need to research, sweetheart.'

'Live your story, as you always say.'

'That's right. I need to live my stories to write them.'

A moment later she made a puppy face and said, 'I will miss you.'

'I'll miss you too.'

'Tonight is our last night together. I shall leave tomorrow. Dad has mailed me the tickets. I don't know when I will be back.'

A part of Kiyan was happy she would leave. But he didn't let it show.

'Make love to me as if there's no tomorrow,' she said and kissed him on the lips. The way she put her hand inside his vest and caressed his nipples aroused Kiyan. They started smooching. Suddenly, Kiyan stopped.

'One second.' He went out of the bedroom. Kashti heard him open the main door and then close it. He came back.

'What?' she asked.

'Nobody,' he replied.

He started kissing her on her breasts. She kept pushing his head downward and was about to guide him to where she was wet when he stopped again.

'Damn,' Kiyan said and went out. Once again, Kashti heard him open the main door, lock it and come back. She was irked but chose to let it go once he was back. She pushed him down on the bed, removed her T-shirt and rode him. She pinned his hands on top and was kissing his chest when he cried out, 'What the fuck is this!

Excuse me.' Kiyan left the bedroom, but when he came back this time, he noticed Kashti had worn her T-shirt.

'I'm sorry. But the doorbell distracted me.'

'If you are not in the mood, you can tell me, Kiyan, but don't give lame excuses. Especially not now, when my mood is already fucked up.'

'I'm not making lame excuses. You heard the doorbell too. Who rings the bell so many times, that too at this hour, and runs away?'

'What are you talking about? I didn't hear the bell ringing.'

Kiyan presumed Kashti was joking. But her expression told him she was not.

21

'What are you saying? You didn't hear the doorbell?' Kiyan asked, freaked out.

'I didn't. Why would I lie to you?' Kashti said, moving to one side of the bed and putting a pillow under her head.

'That's strange,' Kiyan said and wondered, *was it Anaysha? But why wouldn't Kashti hear the doorbell?*

'I think we should just sleep,' she said.

Kashti lay down, switching off the bedside lamp. Kiyan followed suit. When he was sure Kashti was asleep, he checked his phone and realized there was a message from an unknown number. He read the number and knew it was from Anaysha. He recollected Kashti had deleted her number. It read,

All good?

Tina committed suicide, Kiyan replied.

OMG. Is the reason for the suicide the obvious?

Yes.

Hmm. What do we do now?

I've no idea.

Did you get any more information from Kashti?

She doesn't know the guy. Yet.

Let's meet tomorrow. The same way we did. I will wait for you in an Ola cab near Tower A.

Okay. BTW, did you just ring the doorbell?

What? No. Why would I? What happened?

Nothing. See you tomorrow.

Kiyan deleted all the messages at once. He wondered at what a fool he had been to have broken up with Anaysha. He had always known she loved him, but hadn't realized her love for him was so great and that she was so magnanimous that she would overlook the shit he had pulled. He felt both blessed and doomed—blessed because he had Anaysha and doomed because their separation was his doing.

The next day Kashti skipped school. She told Kiyan she would rest at home since she was feeling a bit sick.

'When is your flight?'

'It's at 3 a.m. tomorrow morning. I thought it was 3 p.m. I goofed up.'

'Doesn't matter. So, I have to meet Natasha.'

'Cyber Hub?'

'Yes.'

'Okay. I'll be home. Come soon, hon.'

'Of course. The moment I'm done.'

'Don't wear green. Wear the black T-shirt and blue jeans.'

Kiyan gave her a look, wondering when he would be rid of this controlling shit.

'Sure.'

He doffed the green T-shirt and donned the black one along with the blue jeans. Once he was ready, Kashti sucked her cheeks in sexily and said, 'Come here.'

Kiyan knew what happened when she sucked her cheeks in. As he came close, she gave him a quick smooch and then held him tight, biting him hard on the neck.

'Ouch, was that necessary?' he said.

Kashti smiled and said, 'Absolutely.' She took out her phone and posed with him for a selfie. She clicked it and showed it to Kiyan.

'The sexiest couple, what say?'

Kiyan looked at the selfie. His hair was ruffled, she looked slightly dishevelled and the bed sheet in the background was all scrunched up.

'Don't you think the picture is a bit misleading?' he asked

'It only says we made out just now. What's so wrong with that?' Kashti said, and before Kiyan realized it, the picture was on their page on Facebook and Instagram with the tag 'Doesn't black suit him?'

Kiyan knew he couldn't fight with her yet. He swallowed his anger and left. He went to Starbucks, gave his phone to Rahul and then waited for Anaysha by Tower A. She reached in a couple of minutes.

Kiyan got into the cab and gave the driver a nearby destination.

'Hi.'

'Hi. Anything yet?'

'Nothing,' Kiyan said and quickly told her how Kashti's mother had called last night.

'I was wondering if we could track down her parents' phone numbers. Then we can cross-check if Tina really is dead or not.'

'You mean she would have lied about it?'

'Honestly, Kashti isn't someone from whom I get good vibes. We may as well be safe rather than sorry.'

'Hmm.' Kiyan knew Anaysha had a valid point.

'I'll have to get it before she leaves for the US.'

'She is leaving?'

'Yes. She has a flight later tonight.'

Kiyan realized Anaysha was lost in thought.

'What are you thinking?'

'If I was in her place, I wouldn't have ever left you, especially when I knew your ex was your next-door neighbour.'

'More so if the girl is as possessive as Kashti,' Kiyan added.

'Exactly. I feel there is more to this.'

Kiyan was about to say something when he was interrupted by Anaysha's phone ringing.

'Yes Rahul. Oh, okay. We will be there soon,' Anaysha said, sounding slightly panicked.

'Kashti called thrice. Rahul didn't pick up.'

'Shit!'

He asked the driver to turn the car around.

'I'll drop you off before we enter Cyber Hub lest she notices us together,' Kiyan said. Anaysha nodded.

He dropped off Anaysha and got down himself at some distance from Starbucks. He was careful to ensure Kashti wasn't around. If he knew her well, then he was sure Kashti would be coming over to Starbucks any moment. He walked briskly towards the coffee shop. He was about to enter when he stopped. He couldn't move. His jaw slowly dropped open. Tina Awasthi was standing at some distance from him. He could never mistake her for someone else. It was her. She looked exactly the same. He couldn't breathe. Kiyan felt someone pull at his hand.

'Where were you, Kiyan?'

Kiyan turned around to see Kashti. He mumbled, trying to find the right words.

'What?' Kashti asked impatiently.

Kiyan looked back but there was no sign of Tina. As he faced Kashti again, he noticed she was wearing the same dress he had seen Tina in seconds ago.

***

Anaysha's Diary

Every time I meet Kiyan since I learnt about how Kashti has trapped him I ask myself why I'm even helping him. Why am I bothered? This is the same guy who dumped me because of Kashti, the same guy because of whom I was humiliated by my family, the guy who didn't think twice before giving in to the advances of another girl after being supposedly invested in me emotionally for half a decade. It's not only he who had options. I too had options. There were guys who hit on me in office, college friends who always liked me but never could confess. There were also times when I felt the urge to experience someone else other than Kiyan. The urge stemmed from curiosity to know if love feels different with different people or if it's always the same and only our interpretation of it changes. The bottom line, however, is that I never gave in to this urge of mine because I never wanted to cheat on him. We are humans. We all have polygamous instincts. But because we are humans, shouldn't we know how to control those instincts?

I kept thinking about me helping him, and I had no answer except for the fact that perhaps I still love him. I don't know what he thought when I came forward to help him, but I felt both good and bad about it. Good because I was once again able to help the person I love, and bad because I know the guy I was doing it for didn't live up to my expectations of him. Kiyan said he was trapped, but honestly, he himself walked into it. Kashti didn't ask him to sleep with her. He was seduced. When a committed man or woman is seduced, it can either be natural vulnerability to be lured or because they don't love their partner. And now, perhaps he is clinging to me because he wants to get out of this mess. Am I thinking too much? I'm so confused. When you are in a relationship with someone, you create mini versions of yourself within you. I feel like I have a Kiyan loyalist as well as a Kiyan hater within me. The loyalist in me says Kiyan is innocent. He couldn't resist the advances of a sexy girl like Kashti. Any guy would probably give in. It doesn't mean he doesn't love me. But at the same time, the hater in me shouts out that once a cheat, always a cheat. What's the guarantee he won't slip up if another girl comes along? I was sorted about my stand till Kiyan told me about the birth certificate. The loyalist told me we could still be together again if we could take care of Kashti. And the hater made me tell him that I would go away from his

life once this situation is resolved. Oh
God! Kiyan, why did you have to give in to
Kashti? Why? On one hand, we keep pushing
air into the balloon of love and on the
other hand it only takes a tiny pin of
lust to burst it all. Seriously?

I shouldn't have asked Kiyan about Tina
Awasthi. He told me he was honest with Tina
about his relationship status. He told
me that he told her he was committed and
not interested. After that, if someone is
mentally disturbed about it, then one can't
blame Kiyan for it. So, before Kashti, he
did stand up as the man I thought he was.
But with Kashti he turned to be a man I
loathe. And now I'm confused which one I
should be with or be without.

22

'I asked you something,' Kashti said. Kiyan tried but couldn't talk. He kept gaping at her dress.

'What are you looking at?'

Kiyan remained rooted to the spot, staring.

'Kiyan!' Kashti shook him by the shoulder.

'Nothing, nothing. I went to the loo. They don't have one inside Starbucks here.'

'Okay. And why didn't you take my calls? Where's your phone? It tells me it's inside Starbucks.'

'It is. I forgot it there. Let's collect it first.' Kiyan went in, avoiding eye contact with her. He was shocked at what he had just seen. *Seen? How could he see a dead person? But he had. Was he hallucinating?*

Kiyan walked to his seat and found another customer in it. Kashti was right behind him. He approached Rahul at the counter and said, 'Excuse me, did you find a phone on that table? I forgot it there.' He looked at Rahul knowingly, subtly signalling that he should play along.

'Yes sir, I did. Here . . .' He took it out from his pocket and gave it to Kiyan. As Kiyan took it, Kashti said, 'Hold your hands out straight.'

'What?'

'Just lift your hand and hold it straight.'

Kiyan did so, fully aware that people were looking at him.

'Why is your hand shaking?' she asked.

'What? I don't know,' Kiyan said, realizing it was the truth.

'Are you all right?'

'Let's go home,' he said.

'Yeah, let's go home. I was anyway missing you,' Kashti said and booked a cab from her phone.

'Done.' She put her arm around his waist. Together they left Starbucks.

Kashti was looking straight ahead for the cab while Kiyan was looking around. A couple of minutes later when they reached Tower A, Kiyan noticed Anaysha. He felt uncomfortable and instantly loosened Kashti's grip on his waist.

'What happened?' she asked.

'Call the driver,' he said.

'Yeah, okay.'

As Kashti spoke to the cab driver to tell him where they were, Kiyan looked at Anaysha. He wanted to tell her what he had seen a few minutes ago. *But how?* He would have to wait till Kashti left India. Anaysha too noticed him but had to behave as if she hadn't. She walked away.

Once home, Kashti preferred silence over words. They smoked hookah and listened to some slow songs in a dark room with curtains drawn. She had her head on his lap all the while. Kashti was lost in the songs, while Kiyan kept thinking of Tina. Even the shoes had been similar. How could that be possible? *Some weird game is being played with me*, Kiyan thought.

Kashti received a call. When she talked, he understood it was her parents on the other end. The thought that Tina wasn't dead and the two sisters were in cahoots kept going round and round in his head and made the hair on his nape rise up. He knew he would have to get her parents' number to confirm the news.

'Okay, bye Mom.' Kashti was done talking.

She kept the phone on her stomach and continued taking puffs from the hookah.

'Do leave your parents' number with me,' Kiyan said, trying to be assertive but coming across as slightly unsure. Kashti looked up at him.

'Are you going to ask them for my hand in marriage?'

That was an unnecessary joke, Kiyan thought, but cracked another, 'I will soon.'

'Are you mad? I'm not even 18. Let's date for some years.'

'Of course. But you will fly to the US later tonight. And I need to have a backup number to get in touch with you in case yours doesn't work.'

'Kiyan, I haven't told them about you. So please don't call without letting me know. I'll tell them when the time is right.'

Very suspicious, Kiyan thought. *Like you told me your real age when the time was right. Like I didn't tell you I was committed even when the time was right.*

'As you say,' he said.

'Let me shower. I'm getting a headache.'

He watched her turn the music system off with the remote and amble to the bathroom. With her phone. Like always.

I'll have to get her parents' phone number before she leaves, Kiyan told himself, *but before that I need to know her phone password.*

'Kashti . . .' he called out. He heard the bathroom door unlock. She peeped out, 'Yeah?'

It took him a second to look away from her bare shoulder to her face.

'I wanted to check our Facebook page. You haven't uploaded anything for a few hours now.'

'I thought I would click a selfie when you see me off at the airport today.'

'That's sweet,' Kiyan said and got up. He went to her.

'Don't look at me like that, Kiyan,' she said. 'You know it makes me wet.'

He smirked and said, 'Give me your phone. I want to check our page.'

'But you downloaded the app on your phone too, right?'

'I did, but uninstalled it.'

'Such a recluse you are,' she said and turned to pick her phone up. Her supple, firm, bare butt was all Kiyan could notice. She turned towards him. She unlocked the phone and gave it to him.

'Here,' she said and waited for him. Kiyan couldn't check the contact list in front of her, so he scrolled down the page casually and gave the phone back to her. She gave him a flying kiss and closed the door behind her.

Kiyan returned to the couch. He played the video that he had just made using his phone. He gave a sigh of accomplishment when he saw it. He had switched on his phone's camera before going to the bathroom and held his phone is such a way that it captured the mirror image in the bathroom. With the mirror right opposite the bathroom door, Kashti's password was reflected on it. Now he would be able to access her phone. All he had to do was to wait for her to sleep.

After lunch, when Kiyan asked her to take a nap since she had a late night flight, Kashti complied. Once he was sure she was asleep, he took her phone and quickly noted down her parents' numbers. He wanted to call them right away but stopped himself. He saved the numbers on his phone. He checked her mother's profile picture. It had all four of them, with the parents in the center, and Tina and Kashti standing on either side. Kiyan would have to ask someone else to call them up to confirm Tina's death. Someone else only meant one person—Anaysha. He kept the phone back where it was.

In the evening, when Kashti was done packing, she came to him and said, 'I don't feel like going. I'll miss you like anything.' She sat down on his lap. Kiyan muted the football match he was watching. He looked at her and said, 'I shall miss you too.'

She smirked and said, 'I know you won't, but you lie so sexily that I can't help but believe it.' She kissed him. He kissed her back.

'Promise me you won't meet Anaysha,' she said.

'Anaysha? Anaysha who?' he feigned.

'I like that,' she said and looked deep into his eyes. He knew what she had in mind whenever she did that.

'Now?' he asked.

'Why not? Been some time since we did something kinky. Let me have you once my way before I fly off.'

Kiyan wanted to say no, but he didn't want to offend her in any way. He stood up, picked her up in his arms and without breaking eye contact, took her to the bedroom. He threw her on the bed and was about to pin her hands above her when she stopped him.

'No, sweetheart. It will happen my way.' She got on top and pushed him down on the bed. She held his balls over his knickers and started gently squeezing them while kissing him all over his face. When she came to his lips, she rubbed her front against him, and taking both his hands, started sucking his fingers one by one.

'I want to keep kissing you all my life,' she said and smooched him, sucking his tongue rather roughly. She broke off the kiss, climbed off the bed to open the last drawer of the bedside table and took out one black bandana and a furry handcuff. Kiyan knew what his role was. Without wasting time, he stripped off his shorts and T-shirt.

'The fact that you submit to me makes wet like nothing else,' she said and handcuffed him. Then she put the bandana around his eyes. She put the tip of her right index finger on his forehead and traced it down his nose, chin, chest, abs and finally to his underwear. She caressed his massive hard-on over the underwear. And then with one pull, tugged it down. Kiyan's lips parted. He was expecting to feel her soft lips and warm tongue on his dick, but instead felt a slap across his right cheek. He was about to say something when he heard someone say, 'I hate you, Kiyan.' It was Tina's voice. Or was it Tina herself?

23

Kiyan thought he was hallucinating again. But the slap was real, he told himself. He was about to call out to Kashti when he felt her tongue lick his dick from the base up. *I was imagining her voice*, he concluded, relieved.

'Kashti?' he mumbled. She responded in a muffled voice. He felt her kissing his abs and coming up. Finally he felt her lips on his lips. A prolonged smooch later, she ran the tip of her tongue over his face and then downwards to his chest. She encircled his nipples with her mouth and sucked them hard. And then suddenly, there was no skin contact. Kiyan was waiting for her next move when he heard a whisper.

'I won't spare you, Kiyan.'

It had to be Tina. Kiyan tried to free himself.

'Free me, Kashti. Just free me.'

'What's the hurry, mister bestselling author?' she said and bit him on his thighs. Kiyan yelped.

'This is just the beginning. I shall make you scream out soon,' someone whispered.

'Tina . . .' Kiyan mumbled.

Nothing happened for a while. Then he felt the bandana being removed from his eyes. He saw Kashti sitting on top of him, giving him a serious look.

'What happened?' he asked.

'Were you fantasizing about my elder sister?'

'What? No!'

'Then why did you take her name?'

It had been an involuntary slip on his part. *Why was he hallucinating about Tina all of a sudden?* He had no answer.

'Answer me, Kiyan.' Kashti sounded pissed.

'I heard her voice,' Kiyan said and immediately knew it was a mistake to confess to it.

'You heard her voice? When? And how do you know it was her voice?'

Kiyan knew he was caught.

'Untie my hands, please,' he said. He wondered how to avoid giving away anything. Kashti released him. He wore his clothes awkwardly, trying to buy time, knowing well that Kashti's eyes were on him.

'I think I asked you not one but three questions.'

'I was fantasizing about her.'

'Are you serious?'

'I've always had this kink of doing two sisters together,' Kiyan knew only bullshit could have saved him at the moment.

'I don't mind your kinkiness, but this isn't the time for that. Tina Di just died.'

'I realize that. I'm sorry,' he said.

Kashti didn't talk to him much after that. And he couldn't blame her for it. He dropped her off at the airport. She hugged him and gave him a peck, but it lacked her usual level of energy and enthusiasm. Once she was in the queue at the departure section of the airport, Kiyan asked the cab driver to take him back to the apartment. Tina's voice kept coming back to him. Had he really imagined it all? Her appearance at Cyber Hub and even the slap? When he reached his flat and unlocked the door, he couldn't close the main door. The fact that he was alone in this flat scared him. What if he heard Tina's voice again when he closed his eyes to sleep? Kiyan exited the flat and checked the time— 2:40 a.m. He contemplated going to a hotel. The door across the hall caught his eye. Would it be okay to knock at Anaysha's door at this hour? He was trying to decide when he noticed from the tiny gap under the door that the light in his flat's drawing room was constantly going on and then off. Kiyan swallowed a lump in his throat. Was Tina inside? Or was it just a malfunctioning bulb? He gently unlocked the door. He didn't step in. He looked around. The light wasn't flickering any more.

Kiyan scampered to Anaysha's flat and rang the doorbell urgently and relentlessly. His hands were shaking, and his knees felt weak. Anaysha opened the door, yawning.

'Kiyan?'

'Let me get in, please,' he said and didn't wait for Anaysha to say anything. He barged in. Anaysha locked the door. She gave him some water to drink, after which she asked, 'Will you tell me what the matter is? Has Kashti left?'

Kiyan looked at her and took a minute to relate how he had seen Tina in Cyber Hub and then Kashti wearing the same dress. Then he told her he had heard Tina's voice while taking a shower. He intentionally didn't tell Anaysha he had actually heard Tina's voice while having sex with Kashti. He justified it in his head, saying the point was to tell her he had heard Tina. How it had happened wasn't important.

'This is absurd. By the way, did you manage to get Kashti's parents' phone numbers?' she asked.

Kiyan quickly scrolled down his contact list and showed the numbers to Anaysha.

'Did you call them?'

'Should I? I thought if I directly call them, then Kashti will get to know, because she hasn't told them about me. Also, she forbade me to call them.'

'That's definitely a risk, but after what you told me about hearing and seeing Tina, we have to check if she really did commit suicide.'

Kiyan thought for a moment and said, 'Can you make the call?'

'Me?'

'You remember we used to have another SIM card because we switched networks?'

We used to have a lot of things between us, Anaysha thought but said aloud, 'I do.'

'Let's call from that number. I'll change the name on Truecaller to Telecaller. You make the call as a telecaller asking for Tina. We should get our information then.'

'But they must have a US number, right?' Anaysha asked.

'Didn't you notice?'

She checked the number. It was an Indian number.

'They haven't changed it yet?'

'They didn't go there with the thought of shifting.'

'Oh, I see.' Anaysha thought for some time and then said, 'Should we call now? Won't they be sleeping?'

'They are in the US. The time difference means they'll be awake.'

'How silly of me!' Anaysha said and called the number.

'It's ringing,' she said. A second later, it was picked up. Kiyan was surprised at how convincing Anaysha sounded as a sales person. Half a minute later, the call ended.

'It was her father,' Anaysha paused for a second and said, 'Tina is indeed no more.'

'What's happening, Anaysha?' Kiyan said, and covered his face with his hands. Anaysha thought hard. There was silence for a few minutes, after which she spoke, 'You know where Tina lived, right?'

Kiyan nodded.

'Should we try breaking in to her house?'

Kiyan hadn't expected such a solution from Anaysha. She had never been adventurous. But it told him how desperately she wanted to get him out of the mess. He felt like hugging and kissing her, and staying with her forever.

'I'm sorry for everything, Anu,' he said. She kept looking at him, feeling the way she used to before they would make love. Kiyan came a little closer. She knew what he had in mind. The question was, did she have the same thing in mind? The closer he came, the more she realized how much she had missed him these last few months. She could feel his breath on her lips now. She felt her lips part. He was about to kiss her when Anaysha pulled away at the last second.

'I don't feel like it,' she lied. He had allowed himself to be lured by a girl. Now he couldn't have her whenever he wanted. He would have her when she wanted it. If at all. She stood up and went to stand by the drawing room window. A silent minute later, Kiyan said, 'Are you sure?'

'Yes, I'm sure I don't feel like it.'

'No, I meant, are you sure we should break in?' Kiyan clarified.

Anaysha glanced at Kiyan, urging herself to give him a clue that the kiss that could have happened still meant something to her. Why else would she be so flustered by Kiyan's closeness?

'Sorry. Yes, I'm sure. We may get some clue about Kashti, more than about Tina. As long as we don't know

227

why Kashti is after you, we don't know what she is going to do or doing.'

Kiyan knew she had a point. To understand if he was really hallucinating or being manipulated by Kashti, they would have to find out more about her. The flat he was living in with her had nothing.

'But the question is, how do we break in to someone's flat without raising an alarm?' Anaysha asked.

'We need a fake but convincing story to get the keys,' Kiyan said.

'What do you mean?'

'I have been there before.'

'To Tina's place?'

'Yes. She would have house parties for our colleagues. And she used to keep spare keys with the old lady who was her neighbour.'

'Hmm. I'll leave it up to you to come up with the fake but convincing story.'

'Okay.'

'Let's go there first thing tomorrow morning.'

'Sure,' Kiyan said and asked, 'May I stay here till the morning, if you don't mind.'

You still stay in my heart, Kiyan. I hope you know that, Anaysha mused and said, 'Fine.' She went to the bedroom and closed the door.

The next morning, Anaysha took leave from office, and together with Kiyan went to Tina's apartment. The guard stopped them.

'Sorry sir, the society people have become strict. Please write your name here.'

Kiyan made an entry and went ahead. Anaysha was about to follow him when the guard said, 'But he is Gulshan saab.' He had a frown on his face.

'What?' Anaysha said, and checked the register.

'He used to write Gulshan Sharma when he came here before.'

Anaysha read the register and looked up at the guard.

'Gulshan is his nickname,' she said and noticed Kiyan had written his name as Anurag Sharma.

'Acha, theek hai madam,' the guard said.

'Any problem?' Kiyan turned around, a few steps ahead.

Anaysha stood there, confused.

24

Anaysha caught up with Kiyan and asked, 'Why did you write a false name in the register?'

Kiyan gave her a sharp glance and said, 'Of course we don't want anyone to be able to track us, right?'

'Right,' Anaysha said thoughtfully, not knowing why she didn't want to believe him. *But did he write a false name, Gulshan Sharma, earlier too when he visited Tina?* she wondered.

They took the stairs to the flat that Kiyan said was Tina's. Kiyan went straight to the neighbour's flat. They had rehearsed the story twice. Kiyan would introduce Anaysha as Tina's sister. Anaysha would keep talking to her while Kiyan would request for the keys, go inside Tina's flat on the pretext of taking out a bag, search the place for possible clues and then come out, saying the bag they were looking for wasn't there.

The old lady opened the door on the third ring.

'How nice to see you,' she said, looking at Kiyan.

'Hello aunty. How are you? This is Tina's sister,' he said.

'She is her sister too?' the old lady asked.

'Yes,' Kiyan said and understood she must be referring to Kashti when she said 'too'.

'Hello aunty.' Anaysha played along.

'Hello beta. Good to meet you.'

'Actually, aunty, she needs a bag that's in the flat.'

'So?'

Kiyan and Anaysha exchanged a quick glance.

'So, if you could give us the keys please.'

The old lady looked from Kiyan to Anaysha and said, 'Where is Tina?'

She sounded doubtful. Anaysha hoped Kiyan wouldn't tell her about Tina's death. It would only make them look shadier.

'She is in the US,' Kiyan said.

'I'm really sorry. Unless she asks me herself I can't hand over the keys to you or anyone.'

Before Kiyan could attempt to convince her, the lady closed the door on his face. Kiyan wanted to ring the doorbell again but Anaysha stopped him. There was no point in confirming the old lady's doubts. They decided to leave.

Once in the elevator, she said, 'We should have realized it was stupid of us to cook up a story and come here for the keys. Nobody will give them just like that.'

'Hmm. We were just trying our luck anyway. What do we do now?'

'I don't know.'

They were quiet all throughout their way back to their apartment.

'You can come in if you want to. I'll make tea,' Anaysha said once they were on their floor. He had left his phone in Anaysha's flat itself lest he was tracked. He checked and noticed there were no calls or messages from Kashti yet.

'Sure.'

They went in. Anaysha prepared two cups of tea and brought them to Kiyan, only to see that he had dozed off on the couch. She kept the cups on the table and kept staring at him. She wished she knew what was going on in his head. Once they had sorted out the Tina–Kashti mess, would he come back to her? Would he propose to her again, and if so, would they actually get engaged and married this time? Should she base her decision on his past actions and reject him, or should she accept everything and start afresh?

Kiyan's phone rang, waking him up. Anaysha hurriedly looked away and focussed on her teacup. Kiyan took the call and kept listening. The way he talked, Anaysha could guess whose call it was. He cut the line and smiled, saying, 'Problem solved.'

25

'What happened?' Anaysha asked. 'Kashti called. She has reached Germany. In transit,' he said.

'I understood. How is the problem solved?'

'Kashti told me that she felt restless in the flight the whole time, thinking of how close we were.'

'So she was insecure.'

'Sounded like it.'

'No girl in her place would have left her boyfriend living this close to his ex,' Anaysha said once more and thought, *especially if the girl had snatched away the ex's boyfriend.*

'So, she said I should go to Tina's place and stay there till she comes back. And as proof, I need to send her a selfie from Tina's drawing room,' Kiyan said. Anaysha was quiet.

'What happened?' Kiyan asked.

'Are you sure it is not a ploy?'

Kiyan was in two minds. After hallucinating about Tina, it would be really scary to stay at her place.

'To be honest, I'm a little scared now. I would be really grateful if you could join me.'

'I was thinking about it, but what about the neighbour?'

'Well, if we go with the keys this time, she won't doubt us any more.'

'With the keys? I thought we would need to collect the keys from her?'

'No. Kashti said she has the spare keys in our flat.'

'Our?'

'I mean Kashti's and mine.' Kiyan lowered his voice at the last part. He got up, went to Anaysha and knelt down, holding her hands. It took her by surprise.

'I'm sorry for all this. I know I'm at fault. I shouldn't have let Kashti seduce me. But that was a mistake and it won't be repeated. Please help me get out of this mess. This will not happen again, and I promise nothing shall ever touch our love,' Kiyan said earnestly. Anaysha kept looking at him and thought, *I will pull you out of this, Kiyan, but I'm not sure about anything else.*

'Don't make this awkward, Kiyan,' she said, extracting her hands from his grasp and adding, 'Let's get the keys and get going. I don't think Kashti has yet understood you are trying to dig up more about her. Else, she wouldn't have asked you to shift there.'

'True that.'

'Moreover, this also proves she doesn't know Tina was in love with you, unless she springs a real twist.'

Kiyan nodded. He went to the other flat while Anaysha waited for him. He found Tina's flat's keys in one of the locked wardrobes. The key to the wardrobe was in the refrigerator as Kashti told him over the phone. *Who keeps a key in a refrigerator?* he wondered as he came back to Anaysha.

'Did you eat anything?' Anaysha asked, and looking at his face, realized he hadn't.

After having a quick lunch together, they went to Tina's apartment building.

'Let me go in first,' Kiyan said, 'If I don't see the old lady, I shall call you. Come in then.'

Anaysha agreed. He signed the register at the security checkpoint and went in. After two minutes, he called Anaysha, asking her to come up quickly. She had signed the register with her real name, but noticed that this time Kiyan had made an entry as Gulshan Sharma. She waited downstairs till Kiyan called her.

She went up and entered Tina's flat without being noticed by the old lady. Nothing in the flat, Kiyan told her, had changed since the last time he had visited it a year ago. It meant Kashti had spoken the truth when she said they had moved away some time ago. Kiyan quickly clicked a few selfies and sent them to Kashti. She called him back immediately.

'Love you so much. Thanks for listening to everything I say.'

'Love you too,' Kiyan said after putting some distance between Anaysha and him.

'Did you check our Facebook page?' Kashti said.

'No, what happened?'

'Check and you shall know. I'm hungry now. This journey is utterly boring. Let me call you after some time.'

'Sure.'

She cut the call. Kiyan had uninstalled Facebook on his phone. He asked Anaysha if he could access it on hers. Anaysha handed over her phone. Once logged in, Kiyan went to the 'Kiyan and Kashti' page. Kashti had uploaded a picture of herself alone with a puppy face and the tagline—'When your love leaves you alone . . .'

Kiyan frowned and read the comments. His readers were sympathetizing with Kashti. One of the comments said, 'For someone who seems to be such a romantic and writes such sexy stuff, it's quite rude to leave you like this.' Kiyan wanted to reply and ask who the fuck this person was to judge, but he stopped himself.

'What happened?' Anaysha asked, sensing something was troubling Kiyan. He showed her the page.

'What is she really up to?'

'Sometimes I feel all she wants is a slice of my pie of fame. Anyway, we shall know soon.'

'I think she is simply avenging her sister's death. She knows it was you who said no to Tina.'

'But it wasn't my fault.'

'I know but look at it from Kashti's point of view.'

Kiyan knew Anaysha had a point because he had thought the same himself.

'We should search the place first for any possible clues that can give us an upper hand over Kashti. Then, we'll have to get hold of those videos she made in Goa. As long as those are with her, we can't pressurize her to come out with whatever she has in mind. Though I am sure she must have them on her phone or some password-protected online drive.'

'True.'

The two started searching the flat. The cupboards that were locked were broken into while the ones that were open were searched thoroughly. Kiyan searched one bedroom while Anaysha went through another. After half an hour, Kiyan found a bundle of A4-sized sheets inside the last drawer of the table that had a desktop computer on it. He had to break the lock to access it. He made a mental note to repair the lock before Kashti returned. The papers, he noticed, were clipped together. As he flipped through the pages, he understood it was a manuscript for a . . . novel. And as he went through it, he noticed the manuscript was divided into three distinct parts:

Part 1: Seduce.

Part 2: Snatch.

Part 3: Destroy.

'Kiyan!' Anaysha screamed out from the other bedroom. *Had she also found something?* he wondered and rushed to the other room.

26

Kiyan reached the other bedroom and noticed Anaysha was standing frozen with a doll in her hand. The kind of doll he had seen only in films about black magic.

'Is this what I think it is?' he asked, his voice betraying his fear.

Anaysha nodded. Kiyan came closer and noticed it was a male doll with real hair attached to the doll's head. And it wasn't a tough guess whose hair it could be.

'I think the hallucinations you are having could be because of this,' Anaysha said.

'Black magic?' Kiyan muttered to himself and remembered how Kashti had told him several times, 'Black suits you.' Did her compliment have a double meaning?

'We need to destroy this doll,' Anaysha said.

'You believe in all this?' Kiyan asked knowing well that he couldn't stop himself from letting the doll scare him.

'I haven't ever witnessed anything like this myself, but have heard a lot about them from my grandmother.'

'Even I've heard about using black magic to screw someone up. How do we destroy this?'

'We have to burn it. But what I can't understand is, why would Kashti keep this doll here and still ask you to stay here?'

There was a quiet moment after which Kiyan spoke, 'Maybe we are simply presuming Kashti kept it here. It could be someone else too.'

'Who? Tina?' Anaysha sat on the nearby bed, pensive.

Kiyan swallowed a lump. Was Tina trying to perform black magic on him before she was taken to the US?

'I think I cracked it!' Kiyan said with childlike enthusiasm. Anaysha looked up at him.

'I think Tina was doing all this nonsense black magic stuff to snatch me from you. That's when her parents realized she was ill and took her to the US.'

'I agree it makes more sense for Tina to be doing it than Kashti, but . . .' Anaysha said.

'But . . .?'

'I don't know. I feel an important piece of the puzzle is missing.' Anaysha stood up, pacing slowly in the room. 'You say no to a girl' she continued, 'and she goes so mad that she starts practicing black magic on you? Sounds like an India TV show plot, honestly.'

'I know, but it adds up too. I'm sure Tina was taken to the US because of all this stupid behaviour of hers.'

'Then Kashti coming into your life is a pure coincidence? And what about those visions of Tina you had?' Anaysha said, as if she was talking to herself.

'Perhaps hallucinations. What other logical explanation can there be?' Kiyan said.

'Hallucinations happen when something disturbs you a lot. Have thoughts of Tina been disturbing you of late?' Anaysha said, looking straight at Kiyan.

'More than Tina, it is Kashti who has been disturbing me,' he said.

'Hmm,' Anaysha nodded and noticed Kiyan was holding onto some papers.

'What are those?' she asked.

Kiyan realized he had forgotten about the manuscript after seeing the doll.

'This is a manuscript.'

'Manuscript? Whose manuscript?'

'I'll have to read it to find out.'

Anaysha took the manuscript from Kiyan, flipped through it and noticed the names—Kiyan, Kashti, Anaysha and Tina.

'It has our names in it,' she exclaimed.

'What?' Kiyan frowned and took the manuscript from her. His name, along with Kashti's and Anaysha's was indeed on a particular page.

'What the fuck is this about?' he said.

'I think we should read it,' Anaysha said.

Both Kiyan and Anaysha went to the drawing room and sat down on the couch.

'We will burn the doll once we finish reading the manuscript,' Anaysha said. A preoccupied Kiyan asked, 'What if Kashti gets to know?'

'She isn't coming back so soon.'

'True.'

'And even if somehow she gets to know then she will never know you are the one who destroyed it. And she can't inquire about it either. Not from you at least.'

'Correct,' Kiyan said. Without further delay, he started reading the manuscript out loud. It took Kiyan close to six hours to finish it. Though he could have finished it much faster if they hadn't paused often and stared at each other in shock. There were scary monologues by Kiyan and at times Anaysha throughout the manuscript. The manuscript was an account of whatever had happened between Kashti and Kiyan since the New Delhi book event. It was almost as if he had been under surveillance since day one. From the photographs to the Pune pub and the love bite to the steam room. All of it was there. And that wasn't all. The weirdest part was that the manuscript was unfinished, with the last line reading, 'Kiyan reads out the manuscript he found at Tina's place to Anaysha. And they both don't know what to do next.' They didn't speak for some time.

Anaysha suddenly spoke up, 'Was this manuscript written before the events or after? If it was written after, then it is a documentation of sorts but if it was written before, then this is a plan. No ordinary plan, of course.' She paused and said, 'For no ordinary reason, I guess.'

Kiyan ran his fingers through his hair, panic taking over his face. *What am I up against?*, he wondered, feeling his throat dry up.

27

'Tell me something, Kiyan . . .' Anaysha said while searching the kitchen for water.

'I checked when I came in. There's no drinking water. We should have brought ours,' Kiyan said, guessing rightly what she was looking for.

'We'll get it in the morning. Anyway, whatever you read, did all of it happen for real? I know some of it did happen, like you not showing up for our engagement,' Anaysha said.

'It did. Word to word. It is almost like I was inside a story and someone was writing it. As if whatever happened since the New Delhi book event wasn't real but was happening the way it happens with a character in a book.'

'Does it also mean you didn't tell Kashti you were supposed to get engaged to me?'

Kiyan wasn't ready for this question. It was evident on his face. He could have dealt with it if it was only an accusation in Anaysha's voice, but there was hurt too. And he didn't know what to do except look down at the floor and say, 'I didn't know it would lead to this.'

'But why didn't you stop pursuing her after the love bite incident?'

Kiyan had no answers. Anaysha went to the drawing room. He followed. She picked up her purse from the couch and dashed towards the main door. Kiyan rushed ahead and blocked her path.

'I need you, Anu.'

'You have been saying that, but every time I try to help you out you make it even more difficult for me. I hope you understand that,' she said, pushing him out of the way and walking out of the door.

'Shit!' Kiyan slammed his fist on the door. He knew Anaysha was the only person who would help him. Only genuine person. What had he got himself into with one slip-up? Why had he given in to Kashti's seduction? Impulsively, he called Kashti but cut it before the call connected. What would he tell her? He wasn't even sure who had kept the doll and the manuscript there. It could be Tina as much as it could be Kashti. He sat down on the couch with a thud and didn't know when his sleep-heavy eyes shut.

It was the sweat that made him wake up. He was sweating profusely. But when he opened his eyes, he couldn't see anything. He realized his eyes were covered. That was not all. He tried to move his hands but found them tied by a chain that was locked at the base of the couch, he guessed. He was right. He tried standing up but couldn't as he felt the metal tip of something sharp on his forehead. His breathing increased as he called out, 'Who is it?'

'Who is it? Really, Kiyan?' a female voice said.

Kiyan knew it was Tina.

'You aren't dead. I know you aren't dead.' He wanted to say more but the sharp tip started moving down from his forehead to his chin.

'Don't move, Kiyan, or the face that so many girls are crazy about may get spoiled.'

Kiyan sat tight, feeling the metal tip travel across his chest, abs and lastly, his groin. It was then he realized he had his T-shirt on, but his trousers had been pulled down to his knees along with his briefs. The cold metal tip started moving gently over his balls. Kiyan's heart was in his mouth. He held his breath.

'What do you want?' he muttered.

'I want to chop your ego off. Unmask your fame.'

'Tina . . . please . . . remove . . . that . . .' Kiyan couldn't feel the metal tip any more.

'Tina?' Kiyan yelled. He heard the doorbell ring urgently.

'Anaysha? Help me!' Kiyan lamented. He heard someone unlocking the door. He felt someone unlock the chain and remove his blindfold. Kiyan couldn't believe it was Kashti in front of him.

'What the fuck are you doing here? How did you get in?'

'This is my Di's flat. I have the keys. And what the fuck are you doing here all chained up? Are you fucking around behind my back?'

'Cut the shit,' Kiyan said. He stood up, pulling up his trousers.

'First tell me what you are doing here.'

'You answer me first,' Kashti said. Kiyan noticed she had no luggage with her. Rage made him catch Kashti by the red shrug she was wearing and push her up against the opposite wall with force.

'What are you doing?' Kashti looked at him with utter shock and pain in her eyes. He had pushed her quite roughly.

'I'm doing what I should have done the first time you showed me your birth certificate. Tell me what this is! Why have you written the manuscript? Why do you keep playing Tina's voice to me? Where is she? I'm sure she isn't dead.'

'You think I'll joke about my sister's death?'

Kiyan held her chin roughly so that Kashti wasn't able to move her jaw.

'I'm not in the mood to take shit.'

'So . . . you . . . going . . . to . . . hit . . . me?' Kashti babbled. Kiyan controlled his urge to hit her. There was a smirk on Kashti's face.

'You look like such a bakra!' she said. Kiyan slapped her hard across the face.

'First you fuck a kid. Now you hit a kid. That's two crimes, mister bestselling author.' She still had a condescending tone. Kiyan looked at her for a few seconds and then punched her in the face. Kashti's eyes rolled back. As he let her go, she collapsed on the floor, seemingly unconscious.

'You better confess what the fuck you and your sister are up to when you return to your senses,' Kiyan said and left the flat. A few seconds later, Kashti regained consciousness, crawled to her purse, took out her phone and took a video of herself, saying 'What do you do when your love does this to you?' She uploaded it on the 'Kiyan and Kashti' page and chuckled, muttering to herself 'We are almost there, Di.'

28

It was around 7 a.m. when Kiyan decided to return to the flat he shared with Kashti. He was sitting on the stairs of the Metro station, wondering what was going on in his life. He was trying to make sense of it all but after a couple of hours of going over it in his head, he knew it was in vain. There were too many questions. Was Tina really dead? If Kashti had him by his balls with the underage thing, then what was the manuscript all about? If she was really taking revenge for her sister then why didn't she go to the police and register a case of rape or sexual assault after they fucked on the beach? She kept saying it was her antidote to the insecurity she felt for him. If it was only fame she was after, she had already fed off his popularity. With what had happened between him and Kashti, he was sure she wouldn't come clean to him now. What would be her next step? Kiyan decided to go to his and Kashti's flat. He found the door locked. He glanced at Anaysha's flat. She was home. Kiyan couldn't blame Anaysha for walking out on him last night. Anyone would have done it. He only wished he hadn't slipped up with Kashti. He went into his own flat, drew all the curtains and stood by the window, looking out at the morning sky. There were no calls from Kashti. After a long time, he felt free. The time he had spent with Kashti had brewed rage under the surface, and when he hit her, it was because of all the frustration venting itself. He knew he shouldn't have hit her, but now that he had, he wasn't apologetic about it either. What she had pulled since Goa was not something an average, good human being would do. His train of thought was interrupted by the sound of the doorbell. He opened the door to find the morning newspaper by the doormat. He picked it up and closed the door behind him. Kiyan kept the newspaper on the couch and was about to turn to fetch himself some water when a page slipped out of the newspaper. He paused to pick it up. One look at the page made him sit down on the couch with a thud. For a few seconds, his mind went totally blank. He realized his hand holding the page was shaking. He had to do something. And quickly. He left his flat and rang Anaysha's doorbell. He waited impatiently till she opened the door.

'Kiyan?'

'Anu, I . . .'

'I really don't think it's a good idea for you to stay here with me,' she said.

Without saying anything more, he handed over the page to her. With a frown, she took it from him. It took less than a minute for her to read it.

'Come inside,' Anaysha said. Kiyan stepped in. She shut the door.

'It reads like a continuation of the manuscript,' she said, standing by the door.

'It is.'

'But unlike the rest of it, this isn't true. Kashti is travelling, right?'

Kiyan looked at her as if he was preparing to strip himself emotionally. He nodded, swallowing a lump.

'God, you mean she is here? You hit her? She uploaded some video, like it's written here? Tell me I'm wrong.'

'I want you to check the last part. I'm not sure about the video.'

Anaysha shot an incredulous look at him and rushed to her bedroom. She came back in a flash with her phone. She checked the 'Kiyan and Kashti' page on Facebook. There was a ten-second video of Kashti first looking into the camera, with her face and lip bleeding, and a bruise around her eyes. She was then weeping and talking about not knowing what to do. She noticed the post had been boosted, thus reaching about 85,000 people in the few hours that it had been uploaded, with a high number of Likes and comments. Anaysha scrolled down the page and realized Kashti had removed all the other pictures and videos she had uploaded till then. So the page had only one video now, showing Kashti as a victim of violence and Kiyan as a bad boyfriend. And a terrible human being.

'What is this girl up to?' Anaysha asked. Kiyan had no answer.

'Just help me, Anu. Just help me. I'm defeated,' Kiyan said and hugged her tightly. For a moment, Anaysha thought she would be crushed by his hug. He was hugging her like this after a long time. She broke it before he thought she wanted to keep hugging him and said, 'We need to stop Kashti. We have to stop her before she destroys us.' A pause later she corrected herself, 'Destroys you.'

Kiyan registered it but ignored it. 'But how?' he asked, 'I doubt Tina is dead.'

'Why do you say so?'

Kiyan told her what had happened after Anaysha had left. Before Anaysha could say anything, Kiyan's phone rang. It was Natasha.

'Hi Natasha,' Kiyan said.

'What the hell is wrong with you?' Natasha sounded like she had already judged him. He knew exactly why.

'I would have told you,' he said.

'Who asked you to upload such a video? Have you read the comments on it? Just remove the video. Now!'

'I don't have the password,' he said, recollecting Kashti had once told him the password, which he didn't remember now.

'Then ask Kashti to remove it.'

'She won't. She uploaded it.'

'What's wrong with her? Negative publicity is one thing, but this is sure-shot catastrophe for your image.'

'Just give me some time. I'll call you back.'

'Call me or not, just get the video off, Kiyan,' Natasha said and cut the line.

Kiyan looked at a pensive Anaysha, who said, 'I think you will have to call it a truce with Kashti. Get your hands on those videos she has of you in Goa and only then we can do something. Otherwise, you are her puppet.'

Pet, Kiyan corrected Anaysha's last word in his head and said aloud, 'But how do I find it?'

'I don't know. Get to her Google drive, iCloud, phone or whatever. Make sure the video and all its copies are deleted. Then we can corner Kashti and get her to confess what the fuck she is after. And why.'

'Agreed. But first, we also need to be absolutely sure if Tina is dead or not.'

'You had Kashti's parent's numbers, right? Last time they said she is no more. Let me tell them I had a talk with Tina today and see how they react.'

Kiyan didn't wait. He unlocked his phone and called one of the numbers, putting the phone on speaker. The next second they heard a mechanical voice say that the number had been temporarily withdrawn.

This could mean only one thing. Tina was alive.

29

'So it was a lie,' Anaysha said.

'That bitch never went anywhere. She simply tricked us all this while,' Kiyan said. Anaysha felt good hearing him abuse her. He added, 'In fact, I doubt Kashti is even Tina's sister.'

'What makes you doubt that?'

'Tina never told me about any younger sister.'

'But how well did you know Tina?'

Kiyan stole a glance at Anaysha and said, 'Not that well, but still.'

'Hmm. The kind of smartness that Kashti has shown till now means it doesn't really make sense to try to make peace with her. There's no point in trying to dig up information, especially after this hitting thing.'

'Yeah. I think so too.'

'It's not you who has to call it a truce with her. It has to be me who should.'

'You?'

'I'll approach her, sympathizing with her over the video, lie to her that you too hit me when we were in a relationship and then try to dig up what we need.'

'Are you sure?'

'What option do we have, Kiyan?'

Kiyan was quiet.

'Or we can directly go to the police and register a complaint. But if she shows the Goa video, you will be . . .'

'Fucked. I know,' Kiyan said.

Neither spoke. Kiyan glanced at Anaysha. She seemed lost.

'Are you thinking about something?'

Anaysha nodded and said, 'All the possible permutations of the situation we are in. We have to be a step ahead of Kashti now or this mess will soon be out of our control.'

'Hmm.'

'Can we meet Natasha? I think I have something in mind and will need her help,' Anaysha said.

'Sure,' Kiyan said and called up Natasha immediately. She didn't agree to come up to Anaysha's flat.

'I'm not involving myself in anything personal. I hope you understand that, Kiyan. I'm okay if you guys want to meet me in Farzi Café at Cyber Hub,' Natasha said.

Farzi Café was where the three met an hour and a half later.

'Natasha, this is Anaysha, my girlfriend,' Kiyan said, introducing the two ladies.

'Then who is Kashti?' Natasha asked.

Kiyan told her what had happened since the New Delhi event.

'Jesus, I thought you wrote erotic thrillers. You are living in one at the moment.'

Kiyan didn't know how to react.

'Natasha, I'll extract the truth from Kashti. But I need you to arrange a press conference. We will have to clarify the allegation that Kashti has levelled at Kiyan in social media. He isn't a molester or an abuser. Else . . .' Anaysha knew the rest would be understood.

'Else Kiyan's career is over as an author. Nobody gives a fuck how well one writes if he is someone who abuses his girlfriend in real life,' Natasha completed.

'Exactly,' Kiyan joined in.

'Okay, I will arrange the press conference. But tell me a day earlier,' Natasha said.

'Sure thing,' Anaysha said. Natasha took her leave.

Anaysha told Kiyan to be at his flat while she went to Tina's house to speak to Kashti.

'I'll never forget what you are doing for me, Anu. Never,' he said and hugged her tightly again.

You better not, Kiyan, she thought but kept quiet.

'Call me if there's any threat. I don't trust the bitch,' Kiyan said.

'Nor do I. I'll call you when I reach her flat. Be on the call throughout. If you hear anything untoward, just rush in.'

'That's a better idea. In fact, let me accompany you. I won't enter the premises.'

'Okay.'

Together, they went to Tina's place from Cyber Hub. Kiyan didn't enter the complex. Anaysha went to Tina's floor and called Kiyan. He accepted the call and pressed the mute button. Anaysha took a deep breath and rang the doorbell. The door was opened by Kashti.

'What are you doing here?' she said, pressing an ice bag to her left cheek, which was slightly swollen.

'We need to talk, Kashti.' Anaysha said, trying hard to sound confident.

30

Kashti left the door ajar and went in. It was signal enough for Anaysha to enter. She noticed Kashti's face had bruise marks. They reminded Anaysha of the marks Kiyan's aggression in bed had left on her.

'What do you want?' Kashti said, sitting on the couch.

'I saw the video on your page.'

'It's our page. Kiyan's and mine,' she said. Anaysha sat down opposite her, careful with her phone. The call was still connected.

'Yes. That's the page. And I'm not surprised,' Anaysha said and noticed Kashti give her a glance that told her she was seeing Anaysha in a different light.

'What do you mean?' she asked, holding the ice bag slightly away from her.

'Kiyan did it to me as well. So I understand your position.'

'You are here to tell me you understand my position? That's it?'

'I'm here to tell you I'm with you if you need any help.'

Kashti kept pressing the ice pack to her face and looking at Anaysha as if studying her.

'What if I tell you I don't need your help?'

Anaysha weighed her question for a few seconds before replying, 'Then I shall wish you all the best.' She stood up.

'I'm thinking of suing Kiyan for violence and forced sex,' Kashti said. Anaysha clenched her jaw. She knew Kiyan must have heard it too.

'What for?'

'I have this burning desire to become an author.'

Anaysha frowned and said, 'So?'

'So, you don't get published unless you have a profile that is saleable. After suing Kiyan, I will be the girl who was the victim at the age of seventeen. That sounds like a million-copy deal, right?'

The evil smile on Kashti's face scared Anaysha.

'You must be wondering why I'm sharing my plan with you. That's because even if you know about it, you won't be able to do anything to stop it. Even if you and Kiyan are in this together, the damage has been done. The video is on the verge of going viral.'

'What I want to know is, are you really doing all this because of what you just told me or is there something else to it? Something that involves your sister.'

'Don't you bring my sister into all of this.' Kashti stood up. Her aggressive stance told Anaysha there was indeed more to the story.

'Let me know if I can be of any help,' Anaysha said, knowing she had to part on friendly terms. She took her leave. Once she was out, she spoke on her phone. Kiyan was still on the call.

'Did you hear it?'

'Yes,' Kiyan said and added, 'I was right. She was after me for a reason. What a game she played only to get published. Unbelievable! Kashti's link with Tina may or may not have anything to do with this.'

'But the visions?' Anaysha asked.

'I'm sure she is alive.'

'I think so too.'

There was no response from Kiyan.

'Hello? You there?' Anaysha said.

'What will we do if Kashti sues me? Fuck, then I'm gone, Anu.'

'No, you are not. As long as I'm here, you can't be gone,' Anaysha said.

Kiyan disconnected the call. Anaysha joined him on the street.

'We have to do something soon. In fact, very soon. I have an important meeting at office now. Let me join you right after.'

They went to Cyber Hub, where Anaysha went to office while Kiyan went back to the flat. He had the loose page of the manuscript that had been slipped into the newspaper. He kept staring at it. Kashti had done all this to become an author. *How silly and dangerous at the same time*, he wondered. Kiyan stared at the page in his hand without really reading it. He suddenly frowned. There was a tiny symbol at the bottom of the page that had caught his attention. And it was a symbol he had seen somewhere. He immediately Googled 'Blogspot' on his phone. The symbol matched. This meant the printout had been taken from a page of a blog, with other elements carefully removed. Somehow, maybe, the tiny symbol had escaped the person who had taken the printout and kept it in the newspaper. Kiyan started Googling certain words and phrases from the manuscript page. No relevant search results showed up. As a last try, he Googled a phrase from the manuscript and Kashti's name together. On the third page of the search result, he got a link to a blog titled *A Girl's Diary*. The blog had the entire contents of the manuscript, written as multiple posts. There were no followers except one, by the name of *Butterflylife*. He went through the blog frantically. Every post was signed off as 'Kashti'. So it was Kashti's blog, Kiyan concluded. The last post had been a fortnight ago. It was a verse,

I come to your bedroom wearing a story,
You strip me bare, seeking sense.
I tease you with my naked thoughts,
And we make love, intense.

The moment he finished reading it, Kiyan called one of his ex-colleagues who was an ethical hacker and asked him if he could dig up any information about the blog

260

address. Kiyan told his friend it was for his own safety. The friend told him he would try and get back to him in a day.

Anaysha joined him in her flat in the evening. She told Kiyan to call Natasha and tell her to arrange a press conference for the next morning. They couldn't waste any more time. If Kashti sued Kiyan first, then it would be difficult to salvage his image. In response, Kiyan embraced her.

'Just tell me everything will be all right,' he said in a brittle voice.

'Everything will be all right.'

'I found Kashti's blog on the Internet a few hours ago,' Kiyan said.

'She is a blogger?' Anaysha asked, breaking the embrace.

'The entire manuscript is on the blog.'

'Oh! This is just what we needed. Perfect timing. Now, all we need to do is make sure the press conference goes off smoothly tomorrow. Before she takes the legal route, we ought to make our allegations. I will be with you. And I shall stand up as your ex and tell people that the video Kashti posted was made herself. That we were in a five-year-long relationship and you never ever hit me. She was after your fame. The blog with the content will be of great help.'

Kiyan kept looking at Anaysha. She shrugged.

'How will I ever repay you for this, Anu?'

'You have your whole life for that,' she said and added further, 'Call Natasha. Tell her I shall meet her while you go to Kashti.'

'Kashti?'

'We will have to buy time. She shouldn't file a case before tomorrow's press conference. It would all look contrived otherwise.'

'I agree,' Kiyan said and called Natasha. She agreed to meet Anaysha with her marketing team. Kiyan went out, ready to head to Tina's place but stopped when he saw Kashti's door unlocked. *Was this a signal of truce on her part?* he wondered. Kiyan called her up to confirm. She took the call and answered in monosyllables.

'Are you in the flat?'

'Yes.'

'Okay, I'm coming.'

'Okay.'

He rang the doorbell. Kashti opened the door and went inside. For a moment, Kiyan felt bad he had hit her. *Violence can't be the answer to anything*, he thought.

He went to her and said, 'I'm sorry, Kashti.'

'I prepared dinner at Di's place. Got some for you here. It's in the kitchen. Warm it in the microwave before eating.'

It was amazing how much concern she was showing for him. It was hard to believe this was the same girl who had told Anaysha that she was going to sue him, the same girl who had planned so meticulously to destroy him.

Kashti didn't join him for dinner. Kiyan subtly kept on eye on Kashti's every move. He messaged Anaysha about Kashti being back in her flat.

Kashti didn't come out of the bedroom. He himself went to the bedroom a little after dinner. She was asleep, leaving enough space for him to lie down beside her. He didn't want to insult her thoughtfulness. One last time. Tomorrow morning, she would receive the first blow from him. Anaysha was right. If they had the press conference first, then they could explain how he had been tricked into having sex with a minor. He typed a message on his phone to Anaysha:

Did you meet Natasha and team?

The response came immediately,

Yes. All set. See you tomorrow at the press conference.

Thanks.

Kiyan sighed, deleted the messages and slept. He slept better than he had in a long time.

He didn't know what time it was when he felt someone slapping him, softly asking him to wake up. Kiyan opened his eyes and took a few seconds to understand if it was a dream or reality. Ten seconds later, he was still unsure. He looked around. There was nobody in the room except for the person who had woken him up—Tina Awasthi.

'What the fuck . . . where's Kashti?' Kiyan shouted. Tina looked to her right. Kiyan followed her gaze and saw Anaysha lying on the floor, unconscious.

'What did you do to Anaysha? Where's Kashti?'

'Anaysha's gone. And how does it matter where Kashti is?' Tina said. She was wearing a white semi-transparent kimono with her body visible underneath. Her hair was loose, her face had an expression of fatal intent and her eyes were burning with vengeance.

'What do you mean by Anaysha's gone?' Kiyan muttered, looking at Anaysha's still body. He called out to her, but there was no response.

'It's time to live your story, Kiyan,' Tina said. Kiyan curled up on the bed in fear. His hands were tied with a chain to the bedpost, but he didn't even try to fight for release.

31

Kiyan woke up with a start. He checked his hands. They were free.

'Kashti?' he called out with a slight quiver in his voice. There was no response.

'Kashti!' he said louder, getting out of bed and going to the drawing room. He relaxed when he saw Kashti at the dining table in her school uniform, eating cornflakes with milk.

'What happened?' she asked, with the same coldness as the previous night.

'Nothing.' Kiyan understood it had been a bad dream.

'Okay. I'll be going to Di's place from school. See you there in the evening.'

'Sure,' he said and saw her leave for school. He was tempted to inquire about last night, about her plans to sue him, but he controlled himself. He immediately called up Anaysha. She picked up on the fourth ring.

'Are you all right?' Kiyan asked in a concerned voice.

'Yes, why, what happened?' she asked.

It was just a nightmare, Kiyan was now sure, and said on the phone, 'Nothing. When are we leaving?'

'I have left. See you at the press event.'

'When and where is it happening?'

'11 a.m. At your publisher's office, in the boardroom.'

'Cool.'

Kiyan took a long shower, got dressed and left. He was feeling happy after a long time. It was finally time to heal the wound of the last few months. He knew it wouldn't be easy, but now he would have the upper hand and not have to live like Kashti's pet. Even if Kashti tracked his phone now, it wouldn't matter. Anyway, she hadn't mentioned it in the last couple of days. He was going to his publisher's office after all. En route to the office, Kiyan began planning how he would propose to Anaysha after this fiasco was over. He hoped she would accept because from what he could tell, she was still in love with him.

He was entering the office building when his friend, the hacker, called him. There wasn't much he had been able to dig up except the exact address from where the posts had been uploaded. Though Kiyan wasn't sure how much the address would help since it would either be Kashti's flat or Tina's, he let his friend speak. But what he said made Kiyan falter. The posts had been uploaded from the flat he had shared with Anaysha. He called Kashti. Her phone was switched off. Kiyan searched for NCR International School's website on his phone. He found a contact number and called up the school. He inquired about a student by the name of Kashti studying in standard XII. The person on the phone told him nobody by that name studied in NCR International School.

Kiyan reached the boardroom of his publisher's office, confused and preoccupied. He noticed a few journalists were already present, eating breakfast or chit-chatting. Some people were setting up a camera and a projector, while Anaysha was talking to Natasha at one end of the boardroom. He walked up to them.

'Hi Natasha,' he said.

'Hello Kiyan,' she replied and excused herself, saying, 'I'll just see if we can start now.' Kiyan felt like Natasha was giving him a cold shoulder, though he couldn't understand why.

'You are right on time,' Anaysha said. 'We are about to start. Any update on Kashti?'

Kiyan shook his head and said, 'Not on Kashti, but I wanted to talk to you about something.'

'What?'

'Kashti's blog, which I told you about last night.'

'Oh!'

'Can we talk someplace else?' he caught her hand and was about to pull her away when he stopped, hearing an announcement.

'Hello friends,' It was Natasha, 'Now that our author is here, let's get started. Please be seated, everyone.'

There was a sense of urgency as people took their seats. Kiyan felt a jerk and realized Anaysha had freed herself. She looked at him and smiled as she said, 'What's the hurry, mister bestselling author?' Exactly the way Kashti used to say it.

Kiyan frowned.

There were three seats in front of the camera, above which was a screen for the projector. Natasha took the seat on the left. Anaysha took the one on the right, while the middle one was kept for Kiyan.

'We will see a three-minute video first.' Natasha said.

'What's happening, Anaysha? Which video is this?' Kiyan asked, worried. Anaysha gestured for him to sit in the middle. When he was seated, she came close and whispered in his ears, 'You came to me wearing a story, I stripped you bare, making sense. You teased me with your naked thoughts, and we made love, intense.'

Kiyan's eyes broadened with disbelief. Before he could say anything, the lights were switched off and a video started playing on the projector screen in front of everybody.

The Video of Kiyan and Tina

The screen is blank for some time, after which Kiyan is seen lying in bed in

Kashti's bedroom. He seems asleep. A woman comes into the frame. It's Tina. She gets close to Kiyan and ties his hands to the bedpost with a chain. He doesn't budge much. Then Tina slaps his cheeks softly, asking him to wake up. When Kiyan opens his eyes, he feels scared. He can't move his hands because they are chained to the bed. He enquires about Kashti since she isn't in the room. Tina's gaze directs him to Anaysha lying on the floor. The frame is such that nobody else can be seen. Kiyan asks about Anaysha, and Tina says she is gone. He gets more scared and squirms.

'What do you want? I knew you aren't dead,' Kiyan says.

'Why did you use me as your creative experiment, Gulshan?' Tina says.

'What? Who is Gulshan?'

'You don't have to pretend any more. There's nobody except you and me. You met me as Gulshan. You made me fall for you as Gulshan. You promised me marriage as Gulshan. You fucked me as Gulshan. And then you left me as Gulshan. But look at destiny, I finally found you as Kiyan.'

Kiyan is quiet now. He has stopped fidgeting.

'How did you find me?' he asks.

Novoneel Chakraborty

'For a guy who is this cunning, that's a stupid question. You are famous now, Kiyan Roy. Moreover, that's besides the point. I want you to explain why you did what you did to me.'

Kiyan looks around, looking cornered. The he speaks.

'I'd resigned from my job after my story idea was accepted by my publisher. I wanted to be an author.'

'You had an idea,' Tina says with cold intent in her voice. 'But when you sat down to write, you knew you weren't creative enough to write the character credibly. You needed it to happen to you in real life. And for that, you created a fake identity as Gulshan.'

Kiyan nodded and said, 'You were my subject, Tina. I wanted to live the story I was writing to evoke real reactions and understand real complications.'

'Live the story . . . like you always say in your interviews.'

'Whatever I did to you, with you, told you and made you believe was because my character had to go through it. And the way you reacted to it in real life became the reaction of my character in my trilogy. But I never harmed you.'

'Never harmed me? Really? You didn't realize I was real, my love for you was real, my emotions were real? You came into my life, and like a fool, I fell for you. Then you disappeared just like that. Your readers think you are a recluse, but you tell me, are you really one?'

'I chose not to be on social media till the books became a hit.'

'Of course. After fame kissed you, even if I told the world what you did to me, nobody would have believed me. Everyone would have laughed at me and thought I was a pathetic bitch. People would have believed I was cooking up a bullshit story just to be a part of your fame.'

'I didn't mean any harm, Tina. It was just . . .'

'You promised me marriage, damn it! Every time you slept with me, you promised me a future. Every time you devoured me in your filthy ways, you promised me togetherness. Every time you made me let go of a prospect chosen by my parents, you promised me your companionship. You fucked with my feelings because you wanted the real me to become your fictional character.'

'I know I'm guilty of it all. I did mislead you, and that too consciously, but please understand it was all . . .'

'Let me complete—research for you. I was a fucking guinea pig for you.'

Kiyan doesn't say more. He notices Tina walk away, out of the room.

'Tina, listen, Tina!' he shouts. He sits in silence. After some time, he falls asleep again.

The screen goes dark.

32

Kiyan had safely concluded the appearance of Tina the previous night in Kashti's bedroom had been a nightmare. Now he knew the truth. Every bit had been real. *Just like he'd made it all look real for Tina.* Kashti was involved, Tina was involved and Anaysha too. He glanced at her. She didn't care to look at him. She held the mike in front of her and spoke on it, 'Any questions? Please ask them one by one.'

'What's the name of the girl in the video?' one person asked.

'Tina Awasthi,' Anaysha responded.

'Mr Roy, you know that Tina can charge you with IPC section 375 (4) for fake promise of marriage, leading to sexual indulgence?' asked another.

Yes I know, Kiyan thought but didn't answer.

'Did you think twice before getting into a real relationship with Tina for fiction's sake?'

All I thought was that it was the perfect plan. No harm, nothing to prove.

'Do you think it is a disease, or you are ready to do it again for your next book?'

I now know there won't be a next book.

'The girl—Tina—said in the video that you did filthy sexual things. What were those? Are you a sex maniac? Are all the details in the erotic trilogy you wrote?'

'Excuse me, I need to go to the washroom,' Kiyan said and stood up without answering any questions.

'He will be back in two minutes. Please hold on to your questions,' Anaysha said. She too excused herself and followed him out of the boardroom.

'You exposed me,' Kiyan said. Anaysha looked at him for some time quietly and then said, 'You killed us.'

'It was all because of my story. I was never cheating on you.'

'Tell that to your conscience, but don't give me bullshit. I would have still given you the benefit of doubt if you hadn't fallen for Kashti's advances.'

'Kashti isn't her real name, is it? It is your pen name for your blog.'

'About which you never cared to know.'

'Who is Kashti? How are Kashti and Tina linked to you?'

Anaysha smirked and said, 'You know Kiyan, after I came to know about this abhorrent dark side of yours, I kept asking myself why. Why would you do it when you loved me, when I loved you? But to this day, I have never been able to think of a satisfactory answer. And that's the worst thing you did to me. You left me with a question that shall forever haunt me. I too shall do the same to you. I hope I have damaged you the same way and to the same extent you damaged me. I shall not answer any of your questions. Your punishment is you will go through your life trying to guess the answers to them. And feel terrible about yourself, every day. Like I have for the past year.'

'Anaysha . . .' he pleaded.

'Sshh.' She put her finger on his lips and said, 'The journalists are waiting for you. Be a good boy for once and be back in the boardroom soon. I'm leaving. From here. From your life. From whatever we built together. Don't try to look for Tina or Kashti or me. We don't exist for you. If you try to dig up information on us, we will resurface and press charges against you. And you know where you will land up then. My advice, just disappear the way you did as Gulshan.'

'Kashti isn't underage, right? She doesn't even study in NCR International School.'

'Didn't you hear me? I'm not saying anything. Keep guessing. Just stay away from us. I hope you get that, mister bestselling author.'

Anaysha walked off. She stopped, turned and came back to him to say, 'I don't hate you, Kiyan. I hate myself for loving someone who turned out to be dark—black after I gave my everything to him, assuming him to be as pure and white as anyone should be, can be, ought to be. Kashti will have vacated the flat by now. So you can go and move your stuff and then simply get lost.' Anaysha's eyes were shining with tears, but she wasn't crying. She turned around and left.

Kiyan pushed open the washroom door and went inside. He looked at his reflection in the mirror and screamed out helplessly, punching the mirror, shattering it into thousands of pieces. More than a reflection had been broken. Once and for all.

Black Suits You

Anaysha's Novel

Dear Reader

I wrote the manuscript of Black Suits You as the events were happening. Parts of it were a result of our (Kashti's and mine) proactiveness and planning, and certain portions happened as we reacted to the situation at hand. I didn't tell Kiyan everything because that was his punishment, just like he punished me with a question—why did he do all of what he did? If you really want to torment someone emotionally, I've realized, leave him or her with a question. Kiyan did that to me when he wronged Tina. I did it to him in return.

I know I could've ended my novel with you (the reader) knowing what Kiyan knows. Limited information. The rest you could have deduced, but then I realized, sometimes the readers have the right to know a little more than what the character knows. I think ours is one such story, more so because I have been to you throughout the book what Kiyan has been to me in real life—an unreliable narrator. Of course, our intentions were different.

I never wanted to become an author or write a book. I was happy blogging stuff about relationships every now and then, which increased when Kiyan told me he wanted to become a full-time author. Since I had nobody to discuss my thoughts with as Kiyan grew more distant, I started blogging my experiences and observations in semi-fictional form, and titled it 'A Girl's Diary', using the pen name 'Kashti'.

The story actually began when one day I received a comment on my blog. I was jubilant because I never thought anyone would care to comment. But this person told me she had read all of my posts and was a fan. My blog posts about relationships had helped her with her depression. Let's call her Kashti, because I won't give you her real name. It is the same girl who later seduced Kiyan because I'd asked her to. I'll get to that in a minute. So Kashti commented on my blog, I responded and soon came to know she was suffering from depression because of some relationship shit. I helped her come out of it over several telephone calls and also a few meetings. After all, she was my first 'fan'. We kept in touch off and on till I stopped blogging, because I was so affected by Kiyan's indifference and his preoccupation with his debut novel. I understood what he was going through, but I couldn't control my emotions. To my surprise, I discovered a website—mixednuts.net—where depressed people chat and, in a way, help each other. It was there that I started chatting with a person called Tina Awasthi. She kept telling me about a guy who had tricked her, making her emotionally invested in a relationship and then disappearing one fine day. I thought it was one of those con-man crimes. But I was surprised to know she wasn't looted of any money, property or belongings. The guy came, made her believe he was in love with her, led her to think they had a future together, had all kinds of kinky sex with her and then suddenly, disappeared one day. A couple of months later, when Kashti and I were supposed to meet, I invited Tina too as we had become friendly by then. Two women can gel way more deeply over grief than men can. My jaw dropped open when Tina showed me Gulshan's picture. The guy who had tricked her was my long-term boyfriend, Kiyan. Had we not met, I would have gone on to live a lie, totally convinced it was the truth. That Kiyan was one of those rare loyal men left.

Nobody talks about moral crime. What's the punishment for such a crime? What happens when someone toys with your emotions for a long time and then leaves you because he or she is not interested any more, or worse still, keeps you by their side and takes you for granted since they are so used to you. Tina and I were the victims of such a crime. Kiyan misled her, and at the same time, he took me and my love for granted. The times when he told me he was out for research were the times when he was having all the kinky sex he wrote about in his erotica trilogy. All of it for a story? And not only that, he was also manipulative with Tina. How can people take emotional investment as a joke? The first casualty of an emotional investment is time. And time is life. Where was the Kiyan whom I had met at the ATM, who was so genuine and so in love with me that nothing could tempt him? Do people change with time or does time reveal their true nature? This is the guy for whom I fought with my family, for whom I compromised my career so that he could do what he wanted to, for whom I curbed my interests and spending, for whom . . . I think it is always a long list when you start thinking about what you have done to protect a relationship and realize your partner made a mockery of that protection without batting an eyelid. The ruins of our relationship will tell him how much I hated him, but it will always tell me how much I loved him. The question I kept asking myself since Tina told me about Kiyan was—what was *my* fault? What did *I* do wrong? I only felt the right emotions for the wrong guy. How do I undo that? I broke down as a person. The same girl—Kashti—who I had helped overcome depression helped me, along with Tina, who could mostly only empathize with me. Sometimes, love remains even after the relationship ends. But I realized that the love that wasn't appreciated, and was slapped and mocked has the potential to turn dangerous and merciless. That love demands an action. That love pushes you for closure. That love convinces you your partner deserves your wrath. That's what happened. I wanted to hurt Kiyan the way he hurt me. Kiyan kept telling me he lived his story. I too wanted to live this revenge. I wanted to feel every second of it even if it meant it would burn me, humiliate me or destroy my other relationships. Else, I wouldn't have been able to execute this elaborate plan.

I can't explain it to you, but in simple words, I wanted to take in so much pain that this pain was numbed. Hence, the chosen humiliation of hearing my boyfriend fuck another girl and the shame in front of family during the engagement. I knew Kiyan wouldn't make it to the engagement. In fact it was me who made sure he didn't come because I wanted to live the humiliation. I wanted it to invade my system. In hindsight, I feel it was better to live that humiliation than believe in the fake love Kiyan would have shown me. It was better than tolerating his sleeping around with the excuse of 'living his story'. All I knew was one thing—I couldn't go on with life knowing

Kiyan was living a false one right beside me, pretending he had never hurt me. He would have never told me about Tina or any other girl who would have come into his life. Infidelity, falling out of love or boredom in a relationship is one thing, but making a straight-faced joke of your partner's willingness to believe in a relationship is something that is simply unpardonable, unforgettable. It was that humiliation that gave the emotional push I needed to get over my oh-what-can-I-do attitude in order to damage him.

Kashti and Tina supported me fully in this. In the last few days, every time Kiyan woke up chained, it was because we were cleverly sedating his food. He slept like a log, and we could do whatever we wanted. It was necessary for us to convince Kiyan it was a dream in which he was conversing with a dead Tina, else he would never have ever accepted the truth, and we needed that confession to prove our case. In fact, proving Tina was dead was also important, otherwise Kiyan would have got to her and screwed up our plan, which was simple—push Kiyan to the level where he himself would confess to all his lies. We didn't want to put him in prison. We wanted to snatch away his most prized possession. For Tina and me, our most prized possession was our trust in Kiyan. For him, it was his new-found fame. It is gone now. It will die out further in the next six months when this book comes out, as promised by Natasha. What does a publisher need? A good story and an author whose profile will convince them the book will sell well. I've given Natasha both.

I know moving on may take time, maybe I'll continue to be into him for some time. At the same time I also know I'm not going to act weak over Kiyan any more. I'll never act weak over any one again. That's the greatest lesson Kiyan has taught me. Each one of us lives a projected truth. So, if you think you know your partner, think again.

Epilogue

The book launch of *Black Suits You* went better than expected. Anaysha was nervous, but she handled the questions well. This was the first time in the history of Indian publishing that one author had written about how another author had written his novel, and its consequences. The publisher's marketing team had done a good job of getting the incident enough attention and media coverage. In fact, a debate had been initiated about the ethics of artists. Who decides the limit one can go to for a story, or is it all, in the end, an excuse to submit to a primal instinct?

Sitting through the book launch, Anaysha had realized that life had its own weird way of adding purpose to the journey. Anaysha had never aspired to be an author. Now she was one. Though she hadn't resigned from her job, Natasha had already started to probe her for the next book. Also, her newfound minor success had led to major changes in her relationship with her parents. They were prepared to wait till she was ready for marriage.

After the launch, Anaysha was back in her hotel room. It was time for the actual celebration. Somebody knocked at the door. Anaysha was quick to open it. She hugged the girl standing there.

'Wait a minute, Di. You will spoil the cake. And it's my birthday cake,' the girl said. Anaysha broke the hug and noticed she was carrying a blueberry cheesecake with a candle atop it. The candle was shaped in a '21'.

'I'm tired of being seventeen. It's time to act my real age,' she said. Anaysha gave her a wide smile. They took a couple of selfies with the cake, and then the other girl blew the candle, cut the cake and forced one piece into Anaysha's mouth, while Anaysha did the same to her. They laughed out loud together. The birthday girl was about to feed Anaysha another piece when she realized Anaysha was crying. The girl turned quiet.

'I understand. Just relax, okay,' she said, caressing Anaysha's back.

'It has been some months since the press conference. I know Kiyan won't dare to reconnect with me or you. But the scar he gave me has become a filter with which I see the world,' Anaysha said.

'Remember I asked you the same thing some time last year? How to see the world as if the past never happened to us? Never touched or affected us? And remember what you told me? How to live without being the person you were in the past?'

Anaysha wiped her tears, feeling a little conscious, looked at her and said, 'It happens because we can't accept that weak, stupid, myopic version of us we were in the past. Deep within us, it makes us feel we can never grow and never deserve anything better than our past. But it's a fallacy.'

'Indeed a fallacy. We are way stronger than what our experiences show us. And I know you know all this and are still complaining,' the birthday girl said.

'I won't again. I promise. It was just . . .'

'Don't explain. I know you won't.'

'Thanks a lot, dear. I know I have told you this infinite times, but what you did for me, nobody ever does for anyone.'

'I'm your fan, dear. And never underestimate the dedication of a fan. Moreover, you pulled me out of a shitstorm too. Don't forget that.'

'Still . . . Nobody would go to the extent you did to help me.'

'Fuck those nobodies. And anyway, I agree Kiyan was an asshole, but he was a hot asshole. I enjoyed fucking him,' the birthday girl said and winked at Anaysha.

'Shut up!' Anaysha blurted out, 'All three of us *fucked* him.' They laughed.

'Tell me, when are you leaving for the UK?' Anaysha asked.

'I finally got the visa last week. I'm flying out the day after. I'm looking forward to studying literature at Oxford.'

'Great.'

'How is Tina?'

'She is well. She will be there at the Delhi launch next weekend.'

'I shall so miss the two of you. So, what next for you?'

Anaysha thought for a second and said, 'I will try to live another story.'

The two girls looked at each other, trying to read the other's mind and then burst out laughing.

Acknowledgments

The way a story isn't complete without characters, a book isn't complete without a team. My heartfelt thanks and gratitude to the entire PRH team, especially Milee Ashwarya— for showing faith in the story and my storytelling abilities—Roshini, Shruti (can't thank you enough) and the entire sales team for working hard and helping my vision reach the readers.

Much gratitude to my family for their continual support, which gives me scope to enrich myself every day.

Arindam, Anmol, Bhawna, Rachit, Reetika, Arpit, Pallavi, Ranisa, Lavisha, Aditi, Paullomy and Sharanya: thank you guys for all your help, support and unintentional inputs.

R: be there. I need you, okay?

Finally, thank you to all my readers for accepting my crazy stories and even crazier characters for what they are and caring enough to find yourself in them. A big hug to you all.

About the Author

Novoneel Chakraborty is the bestselling author of seven romantic thriller novels. His last novel, *Forget Me Not, Stranger*—the third novel in the Stranger Trilogy—debuted at no. 1 across India. The first novel in the trilogy, *All Yours, Stranger*, ranked among the top 5 thriller novels on Amazon India.

Novoneel has also written for seven TV shows. Along with his two business partners, Novoneel runs a one-of-a-kind content company—Act3 Creations—which provides content for films, television and digital media. He lives and works in Mumbai.

You can get in touch with him at:

Email: novosphere@gmail.com

Facebook: https://www.facebook.com/officialnbc

Twitter: @novoxeno

Instagram: @novoneelchakraborty

Snapchat: novofy

Blog: https://nbconline.blogspot.com